I0538416

Murder Creek

Matthew Boedy

Published by Matthew Boedy, 2018.

MURDER CREEK

First edition. June 21, 2018.

Copyright © 2018 Matthew Boedy.

Written by Matthew Boedy.

Chapter One

IT WAS STILL DARK WHEN Lovell came and woke me this morning. He made me change from my orange jumpsuit – for row prisoners – to the white one that all state prisoners wear. He put shackles on my hands and ankles and told me to be nice and introduced to me the guards with the shotguns. They're sitting in the back of the van with me behind the cage. It's the van they'll be using tomorrow to bring the media in to watch me die.

One guard is sitting ahead of me, the other behind me. I've never seen them before. I think they know me. Or maybe they don't. I would want to know if I was riding with Wayne Michael Mathis, the last man to die in Georgia's electric chair.

Up front Lovell looks at the map. I want to ask how many miles it is exactly. I want to remember that. I want to ask but I stay quiet. Lovell told me that if I gave them any problems they would turn around.

It's June 8, 1998. I guess it's about 6:30 in the morning. The highway is empty, except for the Putnam County sheriff deputy leading the way. Momma's buried in Putnam County, so I think that's why he came. That's where we're going. To see Momma.

We are driving right into the sunrise. The shackles don't let me raise my hands for cover. This is the last one I see so it's all right.

"Everything okay back there?" Lovell says as he turns toward me.

"I don't usually get up this early," I say.

He nods and raises a cup to his mouth.

Nothing in Jackson was open. All the buildings were dark. When we left, to keep awake, I was tapping my foot. But Lovell turned around and looked at me. Now I am counting the number of times we stop. This is seven. It is a four-way stop somewhere outside Jackson. I like it when we have to stop. I get about five or ten seconds to look around.

Since we left the prison we have stopped at two lights, three stop signs, and pulled over for an early morning ambulance. On a two-lane road, even a state prisoner van has to yield for an ambulance.

There are woods all around, except for the new gas station on the right. It's lit up and bright. Green and red streamers pegged in the ground run to the roof.

1

There's new pavement and a patch of hay hides the dug-up clay under the sign. Gas is 95 cents.

"How long has it been like that?" I ask. The guard in front of me turns and points his gun because I am not supposed to talk unless Lovell says so.

"How long has what been?" Lovell says without looking back at me.

"The gas."

"Been that way for... what you say..." Lovell slaps the driver on the arm. "About a year?" The driver nods.

Lovell looks at the map again. I told him before we left that how we're headed – east on 16 for Eatonton and then south on 129 – is the only way to get to Murder Creek. It's a wide stream, strong enough where you can't cross it yourself on foot. It's fairly long, too, running about thirty miles. The last time I was on this road I was trying to get to Momma. I bet if I had taken a boat down the creek instead of trying to outrun the police in a stolen car, I would have gotten to her. All I had to do was get off the water and walk over to Murder Creek Baptist Church. That's where Momma's at.

Near that boat launch there is the historical marker. Momma made me read it when I was just getting into school. We would walk the half mile from the house when Daddy was drinking and she would make me read the paragraph that describes how the Indians killed settlers and the creek got a new name. I would always struggle because the letters were so rusted. I eventually memorized it and Momma thought I was the best reader in the school. So much that she gave me her Bible to read. Genesis was the end for me.

The Indians had a name for it – almost as hard to say as some of those Bible names – that in English meant Waters of Life, Momma told me. She never knew why they called it that but she said the man who named the creek was my great-great-great something. She said he was a good man, even if he was a murderer. She knew everything about it.

One day she told me this story about a man haunted by the creek. It was one of those old ghost stories I think that her momma told her and it got passed on and on. The man saw spirits floating on top of the creek – all the ghosts of all the people who died in Murder Creek. He was scared that one night he ran straight from his house to the creek and drowned himself.

"Just another body for the creek," my momma said.

Momma used to say the creek's in me. As a kid I thought it was about water in your ear. But now, after all this time, 36 years last month, I know. The creek's in me like it was in the rest of them who killed. There's violence everywhere but at Murder Creek my family made it a family trait.

Momma told me all the stories about Murder Creek. There were Indian ghosts and slave ghosts and the Holy Ghost. She said the creek ate five circus clowns once. They were traveling though on their way to Savannah or Macon or somewhere and the train came off the tracks and they plopped into the creek. She said you could hear them laughing as they drowned.

I don't know if her stories were what happened, but I think they're all close to the truth in some way. When I told them I always added kid stuff like ogres and alligators and escaped prisoners.

Momma loved that church, too. I loved it, too especially the tall weedy grass we would run through and the old tombstones fenced in that we never could play on. And the gray-haired men and women, country born and country dying. She loved taking me there to hear the preacher, once a month. Momma had to clean rooms at the Eatonton Inn most Sundays. She was against it, working on Sundays, but she was also against welfare. And those Sundays – extra time meant extra money – were for me so I didn't have to live with the shame of a drunk for a father and the shame of government checks. "The first's shame enough," she said.

I told Carey through the wall last night about the ride to Murder Creek.

"How long you gonna be outside?" he asked.

"I don't know. Maybe three or four hours. That's it."

"That's something."

I told Carey all about what I wanted to see – the sky and the water and Momma. When I was getting dressed this morning, Carey requested a memory for himself.

"Tell me what it's like to touch a tree," he said.

"Why a tree?" I said.

"Cause we ain't got one around here. I just like trees."

I waited until last night to tell Carey about my trip. I thought if he knew I might get in trouble. But they can't kill me twice. Carey said he wasn't going to tell anyone because then when he goes he might not have the chance to ask to visit his mother. His mother is buried in South Carolina, though.

Carey's in for killing a cop in a convenience store in Thomson. It was his third strike, too. The deputy walked in on him and he started shooting. Carey said he watched that place for three days, never saw a cop come in. Carey said the cop was there because his wife needed milk for their baby. He laughs when he says that last part.

Since they signed my death warrant, I've been telling a lot of things to people. I told the reporter from Atlanta a little about growing up. I told the reverend about Daddy. And I told the judge where they could find some bodies. That's how I got to see Momma. I'm not a big time killer. I have killed three people in my life. I've done other stuff, too, and done time for that. I was doing a year in Claxton for robbery ("drunk and poor and hungry and stupid" – that's what my lawyer said when he heard all I got was $34.56 and a Cheerwine) and my cellmate was just starting out on his spree. They didn't know then, but he had already killed two girls in Valdosta. He was in just for an assault.

We were two months into his six-month term when we got to talking about stuff we had done. I talked about my robbery. I even told him a little about where I come from. This guy had been all over. He had beat up some guy in a bar and because the guy was the cousin of some police, he got time.

I laughed with him and I think because I did that – like I was his friend or something – he started to tell me about all the stuff he had done that he hadn't got any time for. It was small stuff like robbery at first. He took $35 one time from a woman on the street.

"When I was a kid, you know... it was just easy," he said.

When I turned over to go to sleep he told me he had killed those two girls.

"I buried them right where they had looked, too," he said. He laughed but I didn't.

When people tell you stuff in prison, you don't repeat it. I think that is why we both went on like that. We knew we were safe. I kept up with his case and eventually Tennessee killed him, but he never told them about the two girls he did in Georgia.

I didn't know those girls. But I did know where they were. And I wanted to see Momma one time before I died. I didn't want to tell – him being a convict and all – but when he didn't say anything when he died (he sang a hymn, the bastard) I thought I should. Some things are wrong, even to a convict. And when the killers don't tell everything they've done, it's just wrong. I would have never done it if he didn't die.

I think once a man kills he changes. Not for the good, though. And once a man knows he's going to die, he changes for good. The reverend said that to me after he found out what I did to see Momma.

Rick – the reverend – he's different than the guy before him. There was an old man who came to talk to us every week. He wore the same blue suit with the same white shirt. His hand would shake when he offered it. (We like to shake hands here on the row whenever we get the chance – it gives us something to be elegant with.)

When the governor signed my warrant about a month ago, Rick came and was not wearing a suit and did not even bring his Bible.

"What kind of preacher doesn't carry a Bible?" I asked when I first saw him.

"I don't like to carry around two," he said.

I sat there and looked confused. And he pointed to his head and said, "I got one up here."

He said his name was Rick. I waited for the last name. It didn't come.

"What kind of preacher doesn't have a last name?" I asked.

He smiled.

While he didn't act like a preacher, when he told me about changing, I knew he was a preacher. All preachers talk about changing. It's good when you're changing. But when you're not, it's the same old stuff.

He brought a copy of my death warrant with him the first time.

"You giving me this to set me straight?" I asked him.

He shook his head. "Just something you ought to see."

I looked at the paper. Small, capital letters made my name. "What you want me to do with this – put it in my scrapbook?"

He smiled. I could have balled it up and thrown it back at him – something Carey would have done. But I knew what it meant, even if my lawyer said the governor can still call it off. No governor has let one of us stay alive.

I suppose that's what Rick wanted – for me to see how changing starts. When I told the judge where the bodies were, I was changing. I told him he could stop my appeals, too. My lawyer thought it was a joke. He was blubbering like Elmer Fudd but the judge just gaveled him and then asked me again if what I was saying was what I wanted. I said yes, that I wasn't afraid to die.

Rick told me once that being afraid of death wasn't my problem – it's being afraid of life after that.

While we were talking last night, Carey said he was smoking his last cigarette in honor of the last time someone was riding the rail.

"I'll probably be the first to get the needle. Then we'll both be in the history books," he said.

"You been thinking about it a lot?" I asked.

"All they got to do is stick a needle in me. Like going to the doctor."

Carey says he isn't afraid to die, but I think he is. Carey is good to talk to, though he isn't changing like me. He hasn't seen his name on that piece of paper yet.

I try to tell him about changing and what Rick says but Carey's still pissing and spitting at the guards. Lovell always wants me to talk to Carey about that, but I don't push it too much because Carey is the only person I can talk to on the row besides Lovell. Sometimes he starts yelling at me. Lovell does not like it when we yell. He pronounces all the words very slowly – "I do not like it when you yell."

The van crosses into Putnam County. I'm home now. I was born and raised in middle Georgia and I'm going to die here. Lovell turns and looks at me. He knows. He looks at his watch.

I was like Carey once. I would stuff my toilet and flood my cell and they would take me out. I liked to hear the riot team stomp as they came down the hall. They beat me some, but I deserved it. It was my price. But I had some fun.

When Lovell first came to the row, he was told by the other guards that I was arrogant. That's what was in his report on me. Lovell, though, just smiled. "We're going to be good friends," he said.

I thought it was one of those guard lines – all smiles and then you get a stick in your stomach. But it hasn't been like that.

Lovell's a born prison guard – a linebacker with no hair, uniform one size too small. They wear them that way to look bigger. His fingers are ends of a yard rake, strong and dirty. The only thing not mean about him is his face. It's round and black and probably as soft as the day he came out with it. For a prison guard, having a baby face means you have to snarl most of the time.

When we are alone on the row at nights, he lets me call him Lovell, but I understand that when others are around, I have to call him Sergeant Patterson.

Sometimes I like to run out the title and he laughs. Like on one of those pirate ships.

He graduated high school. I stopped going after Christmas in eleventh grade when Momma went to the hospital. She called the sheriff and all and Daddy went to jail but she got the worst of it. I stayed in that room most days and nights until she told me I didn't have to. She never told me I had to go back to school, so I never did.

I asked Lovell if his momma was proud of him for being a prison guard. He said she was because his brother was in prison in Alabama. He robbed an old lady's house and beat her and put her in the hospital.

"I think she's proud of me no matter what I do as long as I keep people like that in here."

I might tell Momma about being proud when we get there.

The other guards seem to like Lovell. They call him "Sir," which is nice for Lovell. I bet his children – a son and a daughter – call him "Sir." That Atlanta reporter should do a story on Lovell, too.

When I told Lovell that he had to take me to Momma, he smiled. He didn't want to do it – the stress and staying later than usual – but he wanted to do it. Lovell and me are good friends. He said he was proud of me when I told the judge about those girls.

We brake at a stop sign. Along the side of the road I see a deer. So does the guard in front of me. He lifts his gun up to the window and taps the barrel on the glass. Lovell turns around then. "Point it where you supposed to."

When the gun gets out of the way Lovell looks at me. "Which way Wayne?"

If we turned right we would go to Milledgeville. If we turned left we would come to – if it is still there – a house where I had dinner with my first girl's family. Her name was Brandi. I was in sixth grade. Momma ironed my shirt and fixed my tie. Don't know why I wore a tie but it seemed important. It was the tie I wore to church and Momma said this meal was going to be like church – praying, eating, and none of the women would say much. She was right.

"Which way?" Lovell asks again.

"Straight. Just go straight," I say.

Lovell finishes his cup and tosses it on the floor.

In high school, everybody knew about me and Momma and Daddy, so it was hard to have a girl. After Momma got better I started building some houses in Greensboro on the lake. I got some money and that helped. When I was 21 I got married to a nice girl from Gray. She was living in a trailer off 129 with her family. Her name was Ashley. We got divorced a long time ago, so I understand that with all the time I have spent inside, she hasn't come to visit. But we had a son. He's got the creek in him, too.

I don't know how long I'll get to talk to Momma. Lovell said if he sees see me standing there, like I was wasting time, *his time*, he said, I would be put back in the van. I think Momma will be proud I have a son. I don't know much about him. I asked that reporter from Atlanta to help me find him and he said they are living in Tennessee. I wrote them a letter asking them to come tomorrow, but I haven't gotten any reply.

That reporter also said he would send them a copy of the book he's going to write about me and Momma and Murder Creek. Somebody should write it down. People remember when you write it down.

I bounce a little and move toward the window. The guard behind me sticks his barrel in my back. I turn and he shakes his head. "Let him move a bit," Lovell says.

I smile at the guard and I bounce again toward the window. I see the trees flash by. I want to remember everything – the sunrise, the smoke coming through the pines, the smells, the bumps from the road. I want to remember so I can tell Momma.

We all have memories but most of the time memories are old. But there are young ones, too. I will have these last memories for about a day. Before she died, Momma said the future isn't promised to anyone. The state of Georgia owns mine. But my past belongs to Murder Creek because my past begins at Murder Creek. This is how it was told to me.

Chapter Two 1754

JONAH THURMOND KNEW they would come and they did. When he and the other men began to clear the land, hacking at thin trees and then burning the stripped bark and bundles of foliage into black, odorous smoke, the Indians lined the creek's bank, spears in hand. And the captain knew, too, they would come again. And they did, two nights later, as a fast wind of fire that split the small stream and then harassed horses and torched the unfinished fence.

In the darkness of this night, Captain Thurmond, who had waited to lead his own incursion and now was determined to claim this no-name hunk of woods, dug the butt of his rifle into the ashes left by the raid. A screech from inside the black and emerald forest focused his attention.

"What was that?" his son Samuel asked.

The creek, deceptively deep and broad for miles in either direction, was to the west. Neither could see it but they knew it was there. They could hear it. And they knew when it changed.

"Nothing," Jonah said.

Samuel squatted to rub his fingers on a small rock. This place was only a few days from Savannah, but it seemed like another country. Here the wilderness enclosed him. Here the land – the water, the trees, the mud, the small vines that scratched against his legs – was unmarked, uncontrolled.

"Stand up. You're getting distracted."

Samuel pointed his gun into the night and fired a phantom shot. Then he put the barrel on the ground and wipes his eyes with his forearm. When he shut his eyes, he saw the marshes. He missed the saline smell in the morning, the sun rising out of the water, spreading itself wide across the surface while it warmed his face.

A snap ricocheted off the trees. Captain Thurmond aimed into the darkness in front of them. Samuel turned back to the camp. His mother and ten other families had come from Augusta – a group supposedly on their way to the Indian capital near another river called the Chattahoochee to make yet another peace.

"They still think we're going on, you know?" Samuel asked.

"I know."

9

"Paul doesn't seem too happy..."

Jonah turned his head slightly and stared at his son.

Samuel understood a lot for a young man not yet twenty. There was the rightness of settling, of conquering. To some. To his father. But across the water, across many creeks like this, isn't the enemy, Samuel thought. These people – and they are at least that, he knew – were like so many others he had heard about. They were making a stand here in these woods. A valiant stand.

"Why do they scare you?" he asked his father.

"They don't scare me."

"Why do you want to stay – here of all places?"

"They're not leaving. Unless we make 'em."

On their first scouting trip, they had seen an arrow. It had been shot into the large tree just on the other side, the split trunks that married at the bottom becoming the sole tree on the small piece of bank that jutted out into the creek. The arrow angered Jonah. "The arrogance of it," he had said.

Samuel walked toward the creek. The path had now been worn from weeks of use. He felt sweat bubble on his skin. Even the darkness of June was hot. And in a few hours, after the sun scratched its way up the trees and finally sat over the towering pines, it would be hotter. He missed Savannah and her breeze.

He walked past a pile of new fence slats – pine ripped from the forest, a forest being defended. He couldn't help but think that. This wasn't *his* place. He kicked the wood and sighed, knowing what he would be doing in the morning. Only when the fence was finished could he sleep in a bed.

He knelt at the creek and splashed water on his face, keeping his hands as cover for a few seconds. The water trickled past overhung branches and hit trapped logs. He eyed the surface of the creek. It was like a dusty mirror. He suddenly knew he would never see Savannah again. In disdain for this no-name place, in disdain for his late night shift, he picked up a stone and threw it across the surface. Strike point after strike point produced ripple after ripple.

"What was that?" the captain asked.

"It was me. I threw a stone..."

Samuel bent down for another rock and heard the arrow. It had hit a tree somewhere. His father behind him was running. Samuel heard and turned to another arrow, or was it an echo? And when he faced the creek, he saw another in a moment. Never could a moment be faster and still be a moment.

Jonah saw the force of death push his son's body to the ground and he eyed the water as painted bodies waded in. He could see spears and bows and tips of arrows jutting out from behind their shoulders. When Jonah reached his son's body, he knelt and smoothed the still red cheek and then filled the night with gunfire. After his alarm for the others, he dragged the corpse, arrow stuck in its skull, from the worn path, hiding it behind a tree. Then he rushed to the camp.

Jonah veered to his shelter and found it empty. He had set up an escape route for his family, as he had ordered the other men. He exited and watched lit arrows hit the tops of other huts. Dark bodies swam like snakes through the area. Frightened horses and chants mixed and then the latter faded into the woods. By the time Jonah got to the corral calmness had already covered the camp again.

As the women returned from their flight into the woods, cries of babies broke the sorrowful silence. Then two men who had chased shadows to the creek arrived and announced the body they had found. Jonah met them and became another pallbearer for his son.

When they laid the body on the ground next to the central campfire, the two other men stepped away as the captain kneeled. He pulled the arrow out slowly and then tossed it into the flames.

"This is the first time they have..." someone said.

"No it isn't," the captain responded.

He had led a party into new land years ago. Like now, there was peace at first, but after a similar raid, he dug a hole in the wilderness and marked it with a wooden cross. He carved his brother's initials into the center.

While some men dug a grave, Jonah stepped into his hut. His wife sat on the ground, staring into a dark corner. She looked at him and then back at nothing. He knelt beside her and rubbed his hand on her womb as he reached for a small pistol.

Outside some men gathered at the fire.

"How many were there?" the captain asked when he came out from the hut.

Paul sighed. "Too many."

The captain stuck the dying fire with a stick. "How many can we take?"

"Why can't we ask for..."

The captain looked at Paul. "Ask for what?"

"The one who... They might have meant only to..."

"They do not miss."

"Somebody should ride for Fort Augusta. This needs to be reported."

"And tell them what? That we're overcome?" Jonah stood and stared at Paul. "We're leaving at sunset."

"Let's not be too rash..." Paul grabbed the captain's arm as he tried to leave. "It does not have to be this..."

Jonah looked at his arm.

"We must do what is right."

"Right by who? The colony? The governors? This is the wilderness. If we don't go, they will come again and again until we're gone."

"At least let us report," Paul protested. "Give it a couple of days."

Paul waited for the next rejoinder. When it did not come, he tried a more practical approach. "You don't know how many there are. There could be more..."

"Sunset. Bring some torches." And with that Jonah walked away.

When the sun had faded, men met at the fire again. There was no cheering, no rally of words, no smiling. They silently lined up for inspection. Paul broke the line and whispered in the captain's ear. "I will not go. You should not either."

Jonah checked his rifle and spoke to the line. "Paul will stay behind to guard the women. Let's thank him for his sacrifice."

The group reached the creek quickly and Jonah stopped before they waded in. He scanned the other bank of deep, thick woods looking for eyes. They were a cunning enemy. Perhaps, he thought, their plan was a raid and then an ambush. Seeing nothing, he declared it safe and the men held their rifles above their heads and breached the creek once more. Jonah led the way through thick brush. They walked for half an hour when the captain stopped again.

"Half go to the right with me. The others go left. You go when you hear the first shot. Don't go before. Take as many as you can. Then come back here and we'll watch it burn together."

From his side of the camp, Jonah saw a fire. Smoke rose from the center of a few huts with thatched roofs. Crops were growing in patches nearby and horses were corralled across the other side.

When he saw no guards, no people at all, Jonah noticed the silence for the first time. Coming to the camp, he heard the trickling of the creek, the voices of the woods. Now as he stood on the edge of revenge, he heard nothing. The outer edges of the camp were impenetrable. A bird seemed to fly near a tree but did not come out on the other side.

Slowly, Jonah put his finger to the trigger, concluding the silence was meaningless. As he squinted into his gun's sight, the man next to him flailed. His arms flew into the air, his gun tossed aside, and finally his body hit the ground. An arrow pierced his back. Jonah turned around and heard more arrows.

He fired blindly and then scurried to the opposite side of a log and reloaded. He muttered hellish words to himself when he saw one body about ten feet away. Leaving his gun, he dragged the body back. Then he aimed at an Indian lugging a body, but quickly drew down his gun. If he gave away his position, he would be dead as well. He watched as the pile of bodies grew.

Women and children came from their tents, bringing water and food. Older men who walked with canes gathered around the fire and raised their hands to the sky. A dance began.

When the celebration ended, the captain decided it was safe for him to get away. He raced through the woods, raced past the reunion point, through the thick brush, sprinting all the way until he fell into the creek. He lumbered toward camp, looking for Paul. Paul's wife in tears told the captain what she knew.

"He left right after you did. The opposite way. Said he was taking a horse. Said that he might not be back for days."

Thurmond mounted a horse as the women shouted questions. He raced through the woods for what seemed like two hours to find a slowly dying fire. Then he crept upon Paul as he slept. He only awakened when Jonah was hunched over his face. Without a sound, the captain reached inside his bag for the arrow he took out of the corpse by the log and raised it above Paul.

"I wanted you to see me."

The captain stood motionless for a moment and then stuck Paul just below his heart. The captain watched death spread, twisting the arrow to hasten the end. When the body was finally limp, the captain yanked out the arrow and saddled his horse with the corpse.

When he rode into camp the women gasped as they saw what he carried. Jonah carefully laid Paul's body near the center of camp and gave Paul's wife the bloody arrow from his bag. "I couldn't save him," he told her.

As the women comforted Paul's wife, the captain washed in the creek. He scrubbed his hands together and then pooled some water in his palms. He splashed it on his face, tasting its coldness. After drying with his sleeve, he looked across the creek. On the opposite bank, sitting against trees, their feet in the current, were the bodies. Jonah closed his eyes for a moment and imagined the one he could have killed. He saw all of them like that, down his barrel.

He began to carry the bodies one by one back to the camp. He grew so tired after carrying the first on his shoulder that the rest were dragged through the water and across the ground like sacks.

The women watched in silence as Jonah dug one grave for all of the bodies. When he finished, he rolled them, his only sound a few grunts. He covered them with dirt and then tamped the ground with his rifle, thinking of the next son he would have, the next settlement he would lead. Generations marched in his mind upon the soil he saw at his feet.

Chapter Three

TWO WEEKS BEFORE I was scheduled to die, the reporter came to see me for the first time.

I told Carey the night before and he started laughing.

"You really want to start this don't you?" he said.

"Start what?"

"Start telling all your tales."

Carey had more tales than me but we both ended up doing most of the same stuff.

"What you gonna tell him?"

"All of it. All of what I did. Even the stuff they didn't catch me for."

He laughed.

"What they going to do?" I asked. "Kill me twice?"

He didn't say anything for a while but Carey was thinking.

"So you gonna say it all? Right. Well why don't you have some fun with it?"

"Like what?"

"Make some shit up. Tell him you killed some girls and dumped their bodies. Tell him you hid some cash or something like that."

Tennessee entered my mind. He was scheduled to go soon. I could hear his voice – small, tiny – and when he told me how they screamed.

"Nah... that's too much. I haven't done anything like that. What's that going to get me?"

"He'd listen to ya. Ya know... about your son."

"But he already wants to listen. That's why he's coming."

And from the wall came a shot of sound from Carey as quick as lightening.

"Then scare him."

"You mean shake my chains..."

"Yeah. Stomp the floor. Point at Lovell. Scare him. Make him think you're gonna cross the table. He's got to stay. Can't leave without getting the story. So scare him before you start talking to him."

It was then that Lovell came down the row. Carey wanted a second opinion.

"Sergeannnnt... Sergeannnt... Patterson," he said in that girl's voice he uses a lot. When he heard Lovell's footsteps stop he went back to his own voice.

"Mathis here has got that reporter coming tomorrow. And I said he should scare him – jump up and down, attack the guards, tear at his chains. What ya think?"

Lovell couldn't see Carey because the solid door was shut. So he walked through the outer cell door and put his key into the food slot and bent down.

"If he does, I'm going to take it out on you."

"Ooohhhh... Sergeant Scary."

Lovell closed the slot door. He walked past my cell and tapped on the door with his stick.

The next morning the reporter walked in, wearing a red tie and blue shirt with sleeves rolled up and carrying a notebook. I was chained feet to wrists, waiting in the room the regulars get visitors. It's a bunch of tables, with already attached seats, two vending machines, and windows to the hallway.

He sat down, put out his hand, and I put mine up as far as it would go with the shackles on.

"Thanks for seeing me," he said.

He told me his name was Josh Holliday and that he was from Atlanta.

I didn't like his voice at first. It was tight, like a dog whimpering. It always wasn't like that but in the beginning he was nervous. I noticed how young he looked. He wore a small pair of glasses and he often took them off to wipe them with a rag he kept in his pants pocket.

"I see you got my letter," he said.

The letter had arrived a few days before. He asked to interview me because I was going to be the last man to die in Georgia's electric chair. He needed my permission to see me. All I had to do was tell Lovell.

He went into his questions.

"I picked you, Mr. Mathis, because this decision about the chair was a controversial one. I wanted to know what you thought about it."

I remember not responding for a few seconds. He waited. I brought my hands up to the table and stared at him, squinting my eyes just a bit.

"If I do talk, what's in it for me?"

He had an answer.

"If you talk to me, for one, you get to come out here as much as you want. Depending on how much you got to say. They say I can talk to you every day up until your execution, an hour each day. And if you talk to me, I can help you... maybe get your name out... maybe help your name get bigger."

I smiled. He took that as a good sign and opened his notebook. He had brought a pencil because we aren't allowed pens on the row. I went into Carey's routine about cruel and unusual.

"I think it's all bad. If I had the choice I wouldn't use any of them. It's all cruel and unusual. I don't want to be no history maker but if it got to me in that chair the last time, then I'm ready to go."

"When you are executed..."

"When I am killed..." I pointed my finger at him, to correct him.

"Yes, before the state executes..."

"Before the state kills me." I pounded the table, to correct him again.

"Yes, before the state kills you, will you say anything to your victim's family?"

I thought about the worst thing a person could do – something so dirty. I remembered I heard about this one guy who smiled as the gas – this was in Mississippi – came up from the floor. I grinned and said, "I'm going to smile at them. Like I'm enjoying it."

He was scurrying to write that down. I added some more.

"They treat you like dogs in here. They beat you and throw food at you."

I pulled my chains off my lap and tried to rip the wrist shackles apart.

"They try to kill you before it's your time. You get me?"

It was then he looked up into my stare and I added one more final touch.

I kicked under the table and tried to slide my hands across the table to grab his hand. I knew it wouldn't go very far, but he didn't.

He pulled his hands back, leaving his pencil on the pad. He leaned back in the stool and when I growled and gave him a claw with my hands, he fell over.

Lovell, who was behind me, finally took a step forward. I heard him and turned around.

"I was just playing with him. I was just playing." He backed off. Carey was going to get it.

He got up off the floor and fixed his glasses and tie. It was then that Carey's plan backfired.

"Is he going to do that anymore?" he asked Lovell.

Then Lovell looked at me and said, "No. He will not do that again."

The reporter sat back down and picked up his pencil and pad.

"I didn't mean all that. I was just playing with you. It being your first time on the row and all."

He fixed his tie again. I told him what he wanted to hear.

"I'll answer all the questions you want."

He sat down again and I looked him in the eye and said it again.

"I'll talk. If you do one thing for me. Find my son."

He didn't know I had a son. I told him all I know about him – he's 11 years old, he has my name and as far as I knew he was living with his mother either in Gray or with her family who had moved to Macon.

I told him all about how I met Ashley, too. I was working on the houses in Greensboro and she was a waitress in Eatonton. She had some nice blonde hair, curly from perms all the time and she liked looking at me. That's what I told her a lot.

She was the first in her family to graduate from high school. She was hoping she could pay for some college classes in Milledgeville. But three years later, she was still at the Eatonton Grille. I used to eat alone a lot because the guys who did the houses stayed around Greensboro and I was living in Momma's house off Murder Creek.

We went out and I drove her around that college. I told her one day she would go there. She thought it was sweet. Even be in a sorority, I said.

Her daddy liked me and her little brother did too. Her momma had died, too, like mine and so we talked about that a lot. She loved her momma.

We had gotten so that we were ready to get married and all and she wanted to live on her own. It was a real nice ceremony in Eatonton. We had food at the Grille. And she loved Momma's house so much that we stayed there, being close to her family.

We started fighting when I lost the construction job. We needed more money because she was pregnant. Michael was born and a month later I robbed my first store. I was on the run and didn't want to come back home, but I sent her $65. I kept some to get some food.

I came back home two weeks later. I had come in the middle of the night, hoping to take some money and some clothes and keep going. I came back then, hoping if she was still there, I could sneak in.

I didn't expect her still to be at Momma's. She woke up and tried to shoot me with a gun, thinking I was a burglar. I woke that boy up and he cried. I went for him and she did too and we hit each in the hallway. She started beating on me until I yelled out her name. Then she knew it was me. She told me if I ever wanted to see my son, I had to turn myself in. I did that morning.

I did six months on that robbery. She left after I went inside, went back home to Gray, she told me in a letter. She said she never wanted to use that money I sent her because somehow she knew where it came from. But she did – she went to that store and bought food and stuff for the baby.

I was never one to be married. Maybe get married. But never stay married. Momma said it was like a life sentence, only you hadn't done any crime.

After that story, he asked me again about the chair and the needle. I said I didn't really care either way. I told him about the field trip we took in the fifth grade to Reidsville where they keep the old chair. I sat in it. He said he would use that in his story.

By that time, my hour was up and Lovell walked over and picked me up by the shoulder.

When we were walking back to my cell, Lovell said he never knew I had a son either.

"After all this time, talking about my kids, you got one, too," he said. "How come you never said anything?"

I didn't have any answer.

I lowered my head and shuffled along in my shackles, looking at my orange jumpsuit. Then I looked back up at him.

"I hope he isn't doing what I'm doing."

"He isn't, Wayne, he isn't."

In my cell that night, I remembered one of the reporter's questions – was I going to say anything to the victims' family? Rick had been talking to me about that. He said someone changing like me ought to say something. Maybe something about changing. I hadn't really thought about it.

When the reporter came back the next day, he asked it again. I guess he wanted to know if I was going to do anything crazy because he started listing some of things others had done. He said the week before a guy in Tennessee had sung a song – a hymn like out of a church book. I had been keeping up with that one case, though it was hard because all I had was the Atlanta newspaper. I knew he was close to going because he had been on the row longer than me.

"He sang that song until they cut off the microphone in the room," the reporter said.

That voice came back to me again. Now I could see his truck – a truck he said he took off some farm near Valdosta – riding down that dirt road, bodies in the back covered with a tarp. He turns left, veers right and stops. He carried one and then another through yards of woods and found that old cemetery. Robinson was what the arch over it said. He dug up an old grave and put them in it.

"What was his name – that guy who sang the song?"

The reporter flipped through his notepad.

"Hollis. Nathaniel Hollis. He killed six people before they caught him. All young girls. In South Carolina, North Carolina, and Tennessee."

"Did he say anything? Besides singing?"

"No. He just died. They said he looked like he enjoyed it."

He didn't say anything. He could've, but he didn't. The bastard died with two girls in the cemetery. We talked about some more stuff that day but I don't remember any of it. I was thinking about those two girls. It's strange. I don't see Mr. Cho and his wife much in my dreams. I don't see the gun I pointed at them for those seconds. I don't see Daddy falling into the creek. But I hear that voice. I see him digging that hole. I see him walking back to that truck.

I told Rick the story about the guy from Tennessee and how he sang a hymn. I didn't let on about me knowing about the girls.

"Why do you think he did that? He could've said something, like you've been asking me to."

Rick said he didn't know, but it was probably because the man in Tennessee wasn't ready to die. I told him what the reporter said about him enjoying the chair.

Rick laughed.

"You're lucky – I almost say blessed – because you know. You know a week from now you're going to be put in a chair and you will die. You might say that's the worst knowledge to have. But in a way that's a good thing. He knew, too, that man from Tennessee. But he wasn't ready. That's why he laughed or smiled or did whatever they said. He wasn't ready. Being ready, Wayne, that's the hard part. I bet he thought was ready because he had killed all those people, that he'd seen all them die and so he knew what it would be like. But he wasn't."

"How do you know he wasn't?"

"Wayne from all that you told me, your mother was a nice, loving woman. You told me how she lived in that house, protecting you and making sure you had food and went to school. And how she was killed by your father. I don't know all the details but I bet she didn't know when she was going to die. But she was ready.

"How do you know that?"

"The same way I know you aren't ready. When they arrested you, you still had the gun and everything still from the shooting. Why did you go back?"

"I knew they was chasing me... and I knew the house was..."

"But you didn't go to the house. You were caught at the cemetery, running through the cemetery. Why did you go there?"

"To see Momma."

"That's right. To see your mother's grave. You may have thought you were ready. Because you were there with that gun. You were there to shoot yourself and you may have thought you were ready. But you weren't. Wayne, all this we've been talking about – about changing – is getting you ready."

"Am I ready now?"

"I think you still have something you want to say to your mother. That's why you went there. Did you get to talk to her?"

I shook my head.

After Rick left, I thought telling about those girls would be get me ready. But I wasn't sure.

That week me and the reporter talked about a lot of things. He asked about what appeals I had left. I said there were a few, but my lawyer knew better. He asked about being on the row. I said Lovell and the others were nice and that the other guys on the row were good to me.

Then the reporter said he wanted to ask some questions about the people I killed. He said their names – "Mr. Jun Cho and his wife, Kim..." He looked through his notes for something and then found it – "who ran a convenience store near Monticello. They had just opened their store about a year earlier..."

When the reporter started talking about them, I knew Lovell would hear it. He always stood behind me at the door while I talked to the reporter. Sometimes he brought me a Coke, too.

I never wanted Lovell to really hear my crimes. I never talked about me killing anybody with him or me robbing stores. I knew he knew – he had to know – but I never wanted him to hear all those things. There was some stuff he didn't know, too.

"You never testified at the trial. Probably your lawyer told you not to. But why did you shoot them – Mr. Cho and his wife? You had the money in your hand. Why didn't you just run?"

I thought about it for a second. I remembered watching that tape at trial. Black and white security video and the prosecutor showing it to the jury. He counted the seconds out loud for them. One. Two. Three. All the way to 15. I stood there with the gun pointed at them for those seconds and then shot them. Emptied the whole gun into them.

I thought about what I did to Daddy, too. After I beat him a little and walked him at gunpoint to that creek that went through the backyard, I made him stand there for a while before I shot him. I counted that in my head. One. Two. Three. All the way to 5. Bang. To the head.

Rick had asked that same question, too. Why did I stand there? Rick didn't answer. He just left me with it. Now here I was with it again.

I didn't have any real answer. All I had was some words.

"They were scared and all – never been robbed before it seemed like. He was trying to give me the money and hold her, too. They were both real short people and it seemed like I was 10 feet tall. I took the money and I stood there watching him and watching her and him watching her and... and..."

"Did you see someone coming? Did your finger slip?"

"Nah. I just shot 'em. I just shot 'em. Bang. Bang. Bang."

"You shot them 12 twelve times – the whole clip."

"Yep. I did. Bang. Bang. Bang. Soon they all started sounding like one shot with the echoes and all."

He was writing all this down. And when he was done, he sat there for a minute. I guess he was hoping I might say something more.

I tried to turn my head to look at Lovell. But I couldn't. I looked at the reporter. We looked the same age. He looked a little cleaner and his hair was cut. Even looked like he had some stuff in it. His glasses – the ones he was now cleaning with that rag from his pocket – looked expensive and his shirt and tie, too. I started talking to him.

"Where you from?" I asked.

"I work for the Atlanta..."

"You said that. But where you from? Where did you grow up?"

He looked over my shoulder at Lovell. I don't think he came here looking to answer any questions.

"Where you from? I'm from down the road. My Momma lived on some land outside Eatonton."

He finally answered.

"I was born in Vermont. But I lived all over. I've been in Atlanta ten years now."

I nodded my head.

"You like it there?"

"Yeah. Kids in a good school."

"You always been a reporter?"

"Yeah."

It was like we were drinking some beer at a bar.

"You like writing stories and talking to people?"

"Yeah."

"Is your momma dead yet?"

He paused in his response routine. I answered for him.

"My daddy killed my momma. Drunk and then beat her with a tire iron and when he finished with that, he shot her in the head."

He didn't write that down.

"You can write that down if you want."

He moved his pencil on his paper and I could see some words but I wasn't sure if he was writing what I said.

He looked at me after he finished and didn't say anything. So I did.

"Momma said I come from a long line of killers. Something she would say – go on and on about stories of people in my family who killed, who lived around where we live – people who shot and stabbed and hung and did all kinds of stuff. I wasn't making excuses for myself when I said that about my daddy. But when I stood there in front of Mr. Cho and his wife, counting, I think now

I was counting the all the kin I knew who had killed. All the people with the creek in them. That's what Momma said we had.

"Then I kept counting, seeing the faces of all the people who had died. For a few seconds they all seemed to come in me and I was fighting them, fighting with them, fighting for them and dying in them and breathing and killing and dying...I almost stopped counting. Then I pulled the trigger. I shot them. Mr. Cho and his wife. I pulled that trigger. But then the counting and all those people – the killers who lived by the creek, who live in me – who are me – they kept pulling that trigger. They kept killing. They kept the creek flowing. I guess that's why it's called Murder Creek."

He sat there speechless for a long time. I did, too. I looked up at the clock on the wall and our hour had gone by. He saw me looking, too, and started to stand up. Then Lovell came over to me. He started to pull me up and I stopped him for a second and looked at the reporter.

"Hey if you ever find my son, when you do... don't tell him all that. Tell him his father just shot some people." He nodded and left.

I wanted to tell Rick I had answered his question but it was Friday and on the weekends, no one is allowed in the prison.

Carey tapped on the wall Saturday night after lights out.

"You tell him everything yet?"

"No."

"No? You been in there every day this week. What you been doing – talking about the future? That's probably why he ain't got to your son yet. You ain't tell him what he wants. I think you ought to make up some..."

"You ever thought about why you killed them people?"

He paused and answered.

"The cop came in. He pulled his gun. I had too."

"Yeah but why didn't you just run? Or give up? Why did you have to shoot him?"

"Why did you shoot those Koreans?"

I didn't answer for a while. He went back to his plan for better stories.

"Tell him you strangled a cat or stabbed a dog. They love shit like that."

I wanted to go along but I just started talking.

"I told him I shot those people because I saw the faces of all the dead people I know and all the faces of all the killers I know. That they were fighting inside of me and I pulled the trigger."

"You told the reporter that?"

"Yeah."

"Hell, they love shit like that, too. They might get you off for that. Crazy killer can't be killed cause he's crazy."

"Yeah, but that isn't it. I am not crazy. I just saw for a few seconds... I just heard Momma talking about where I came from."

"You heard voices?"

"Not heard *heard*. Just you know... remembered what my momma had said. That I came from a long line of killers."

"My momma used to tell me I got trouble in my blood."

"Was your momma dead when you shot that cop?"

"Nope. She came to the trial and everything. Told the jury how I was a disrespectful brat and used to run around and raise hell. Then she started crying and telling them how I didn't deserve to die. Hell, she knew I was getting the chair – or I guess now the needle. She knew. Hell, she probably wanted me to get it. But you got to love your momma."

"My momma died before I did anything. But she always used to say I came from a long line of... And she always wanted me to go to church with her."

"Yours, too? My momma dragged me. Then when I got bigger I just stood there and she couldn't drag no boy anymore."

"She always wanted me to get baptized, too. They used to do it in the creek that ran near the house. Every summer. And every year I didn't go... Carey you think we shot those people cause we're evil?"

"Hell, my momma said I was born evil."

So was I, I thought. I've seen it. Then thought about Tennessee. And Momma being dead and my son growing up. And me not being ready to die with a week left to live.

I told Carey I was going to sleep.

"Hey, Wayne. That preacher tell you you were evil?"

"Nah... just something I thought about."

"Oh. Cause you ain't, Wayne. You different than me. You ain't evil."

I said thanks and went to sleep. I don't know why I said all those things to the reporter. It's just what I saw. It's just what evil is, I guess.

On Monday I was expecting to talk with the reporter again but he didn't come. He didn't say he wasn't coming. I remember before he left he said he would talk with me again, too. Lovell told me he hadn't come and I just stood there at my door for a while.

Rick came by though on Monday afternoon. Lovell brought him to my cell and opened up the solid door but not the barred door. He was wearing a Hawaiian shirt and some pants. He had a folding chair and this time he carried a Bible.

"You forget your copy?" I asked and then laughed. "You know? For...get. Like you can't remember?"

He smiled and sat down in the chair.

"Sergeant Patterson told me you've been talking a lot to that reporter."

"What else did he say?"

"That you seem to like talking to him."

"Yeah. It's alright."

"You like talking to me?"

"Yeah. Rick, you and me and Lovell we ought to have a barbecue, drink some beer and all."

"He also said you mentioned your daddy."

"Lovell does hear a lot."

"He also said you asked the reporter to find your son."

"Yeah. I wanted him to visit."

It was then he picked up the Bible off the floor. There was a white piece of paper stuck inside and he opened to that paper.

"Maybe this will help."

He stuck the piece of paper through the cell bars and I read it. It was an address of somewhere in Tennessee.

"What's this?"

"It's your son's address. The reporter called over and gave it to the warden who passed it along to the sergeant. Now I'm giving it to you."

"That reporter – he coming back?"

"Yes. He said he would be back."

I sat there with the paper in my hands. I kept reading and reading it. I yelled over to Carey and read the address to him. Lovell made a pass on our cells and shook his head.

"Rick, you think I should write to him? Do you think he'll come if I ask?"

"I don't know. I think it won't do any harm. I think a son always wants to hear from his father."

"Yeah. Yeah. That's sounds right."

I was so excited or talkative I asked Rick what he had in mind today for me. I completely forgot the question he had asked and how I had answered it with the reporter.

"You ever thought about your father before Friday?"

"Yeah some."

"You ever think about how your mother died?"

"Yeah some."

"Tell me about it."

I got up from my bed and stepped toward the cell door. I laid my body against it and my hands held the bars above my head.

"He was a drunk all the time, even before I was born. Momma always stayed though. He used to walk into church drunk but he never made it up the aisle. Momma always said that he had the creek in him. I thought as a kid that he got his drinks down there. He didn't really get real violent until she started fighting back. I mean I guess I didn't notice until she just stopped hiding it.

"He come home one day in the summer after drinking in the heat. I was there, living there. He didn't like that. Eighteen years old and still at home – dropped out, had no job cause I had gotten laid off. He had this job – running trucks or something on the highway. He come in, getting on me about being there and told me to get off his couch. I did. Then he went on and on about dinner. It was in the afternoon. He spills his drink and tells me to get another one. Now all the times I can remember him telling me to get him a new one after he's spilled it, I did. But I sat there. Like I did when I shot those people. I just sat there.

"He come slumping over to where I was sitting and yelling and screaming and hunched over in my face. He raised his hand when Momma walked in. And she grabbed his hand and turned him around. I think she was going to do something but when she saw that face, she froze.

"They yelled and he chased her and went outside. I didn't see him go outside but he came back in and started on her with that tire iron. I tried to pull him off but he gave me a few good ones to the stomach and one to the shoulder and I watched as he beat her and beat her and... Then when she wasn't moving no more, he went to the closet and got out that handgun. He squatted down and whispered something in her ear. Then he stood up and shot her in the head."

I sat back down on the bed. I wanted to tell Rick what happened next. I wanted to say it right then. It was bad what I'd done. I knew it then. Then Rick asked his next question.

"You ever think that you would end up like him?'

"I knew I would. Yeah. I knew. Momma knew, too."

"I see. She said you'd come from a long line of killers. You think that she meant you were going to be one, too."

"What else did she mean?"

"You were good for so many years. You tried and tried and couldn't change. You think that you didn't get out of that and Momma wouldn't be proud. Right?"

I nodded.

"And that's why you went back there, to tell her how sorry you are. To tell her that..."

I got up from my bed and walked toward the end of my cell. To tell her that I was sorry for killing Daddy? No. I wasn't sorry about that. But yeah I was sorry I didn't get out of it – get out of the creek. Or I was sorry I didn't get the creek out of me. That I became a killer. That I couldn't change.

"She wanted you to be something different. She wanted you to go to church and be... She wanted you to change."

I think Rick was startled when I done it. But I stuck my hand in my toilet. I pulled it out, dripping. He didn't say anything. I stood there looking at the water.

"Is this water clean?" I asked.

"I think that when you flush it sends..."

"Can any water in any toilet bowl be clean? I mean you drop something in here, I'm not going to go get it."

"So why did you put your hand in it now?"

"Momma said you could go into dirty water and then when you come up, you could be clean. That you would look around and not see that it was dirty. That you could go under and come up and it would look clean."

"Like getting baptized."

"Momma always wanted me to get baptized. Always wanted me to do it. Cause she said that it washed away stuff, that it made it like starting over. She said Murder Creek had a church because we needed one. And she said Murder Creek was the place for baptisms because it was the dirtiest water she knew – dirty she said from that long line of bodies and killers. So it was good for dunking. I just fought and fought it and then she got in the hospital and then Daddy came home drunk and I had...I just never did it."

"Is that what you want to apologize for?"

"Yeah I suppose. Momma always said I should own up to stuff I've done."

"And your son? Do you think there's something you want to say to him? Do you think he knows he comes from a long line of killers?"

"He's got me in him. He's got the creek in him. All those stories Momma told me about how we killed. They came true. I did it. And he's..."

"You think your son is going to be a killer?"

"My boy's like me. I know it. He's knows it. His momma knows it."

"Maybe if you write him and tell him – give him some advice – tell him what you could've said, would've said if you had the chance."

I sat on my bed with my hands in my face. If I had the chance. If I had the chance, I would've done a lot of things. I would have got Ashley something nice. I would have not shot those people. I would have gone with Momma to church more. I would have got put in that creek like she wanted. I would have killed Daddy sooner.

"And Wayne, on Saturday, they're going to give you some time to speak. You know that. I think you could say something about your Momma then. Maybe say what you want to say to her then.

"There's a lot of people you can make it right with, Wayne. You can make it right with your son. You can make it right with the family of who you shot. You can make it right with your momma."

"How do I make it right with her? She's dead."

Saying it out loud only made it worse. I didn't have any way to make it right. And then Rick made it worse.

"You can make it right with yourself."

I thought he knew then. I thought that somehow Rick knew what happened next between Daddy and me. Cause if Rick knew – if he knew about Daddy, he knew I wasn't sorry and all that made me become a killer which made me sorry for disappointing Momma. I thought he knew all that. I thought, too, he knew how to change all that. And he was going to tell me. Because I didn't know.

"And if I do all that – make it right with everybody – would that make me ready?"

"I think you would know then."

"And what if I don't? What if I can't? What if I am not ready?"

He sat there, and I hoped for an answer, hoped. I am not one for feelings but I hoped then that he could tell me how to do it – how to make it right with myself for killing Daddy. I hoped he could. But he didn't.

"Wayne, this is a lot to think on. Let me come back tomorrow and we'll talk some more."

He got up from his chair and was folding it up when I blurted it out. It was all I knew to do to make it right. I guess it was then I started changing.

"I want to make it right for them girls."

"What girls Wayne?"

"Those girls in that cemetery."

Chapter Four 1804

NO ONE HAD REMEMBERED what Robinson Manning had said or even who he was. No one had remembered that he would be here. But there he stood, like he said, exactly a year gone by.

That day, he had stopped his horse and shoved a book in the air and announced that this town – if one could call it a town – now belonged to God and that one year later he would return to preach and baptize and begin a church.

It was a moment of time – he stopped, hopped, made his prophecy and left – in the middle of a hot Georgia June that hardly anyone saw. One woman was wafting the afternoon humidity from her face with a fan on a balcony of the hotel, one of the three buildings at this crossroads. There was what appeared to be a drunk asleep, his shoulder resting on the post that held the balcony aloft. And a child chased a dog through the street.

It was quiet, but not because anyone was listening. It was an announcement to the wind, to the dust, to the emptiness that was this community somewhere north of Macon.

Manning traveled west, to Alabama, to Mississippi, into Indian land, and then had returned, as promised to the lost of this village. It had no name, no distinguishing monuments except a creek that ran nearby. Now as he sat on his horse under the same hot Georgia sun, he hungered for the same missing sheep.

No one was there to meet Manning and so Manning brought the crowd to him. He rummaged through a bag and strapped to his body a drum. He marched – a one-man parade – up and down the street banging on the drum with a stick until all the eyes were upon him. With his thick head of hair and full beard and tall, lanky skeleton, it was as if Jesus was strutting through this southern outpost.

No one had ever seen a preacher like this.

A handful of people emerged. Another woman joined the balcony, fan in hand. Men began to shoulder posts, elbows cocked. And the child (oh how he loved the children, any child) stopped to his voice. Let them who have ears hear.

31

He unshackled his instrument and shoved a book into the air. The same book – a King James passed down by his father – he had thrust like a weather vane 365 days ago, measuring the spiritual health, the spiritual need of this town.

"Tomorrow, there will be preaching at the creek south of here and many will come. A few will hear and be saved. Many will come and some will be baptized. They will come out of the water and be saved."

No one from around here had ever heard a preacher like this before. It was a voice, unmistakably not from around here. It did not drawl; it did not sit in the air, waiting for the words to travel. It did not settle; it flashed, it sped up. It did not slow down; it halted. It did not talk; it spoke.

Someone screamed "Get outta here yankee." Many laughed and then another man whistled and then the preacher shoved the book back into the air.

"This town shall hear the word of the Lord."

Then he began to read aloud. There was a verily and a ye and an unto and by the time Manning had read his two chosen sentences, words from his Lord about death and judgment and salvation, a drunk man who had been spinning the empty chamber of his pistol had found the dexterity to load and fire.

It wasn't the amen the preacher was looking for. He hunkered, hearing the shot. With what he hoped was now an empty gun, Manning saw the drunk man aim at him.

Manning pointed back at the man with his finger and announced, "The Lord shall be your overflowing. Not that whiskey." The man cocked the gun then released the hammer. Empty.

Once again, Manning raised his Bible into the air.

"Tomorrow hear the word and be saved. Tomorrow you can begin to live forever."

With that he saddled his horse and rode south, to the waters he remembered from a year ago. It was a wide creek with a slow current. Its banks were filled with trees and heavy brush, but he found a clearing just off the horse path. It seemed two trees were sharing the same stump.

It also seemed he was sharing the clearing and its creek with another. A woman was kneeling and hunched over the waters. He slowly stopped his horse but still it neighed and the woman turned to the sound.

She quickly stood and held clothes in front of her, as if to guard her shame. But she was wearing a cotton dress, flowers dotting the length.

He knew she would be scared.

"I mean you no harm," he said calmly.

With that he got off his horse and slowly walked it toward her. He tied it up on the twin tree and their faces were so close he could touch her. As he looked at her face, a taste of cream filled his mouth – warm and moist – a taste of childhood. Her cheek was wet with sweat but it seemed to brighten her face, not diminish its beauty. Her eyes seemed a channel, a watery channel in a deep river.

She averted those eyes, taking her face as well. He let his fingers traveled down, too. He balanced her chin on his pointer and brought it back level with his.

"I am a preacher. I just came through the village above here. Your village?"

She shook her head away. She bent down to gather what was left of her clothes. By the time he did the same, she was erect and walking away. He sped up to catch her and grabbed her by the shoulder.

"Do you have a na..."

But she took off again and he stood there, unable to move another step. He watched her leave, her body slowly taken by the woods.

Youthful as he was, Manning was bold with his audiences. He spoke with power and strength and length and honor. Yet as a man, as a man on his own, still alone, he had never touched a stranger like that. Never touched a woman like that.

She, too, was young. He felt drawn to her, as if she were scared. Scared of a stranger, yes. But scared of the world, scared of the wilderness. Scared and in need – a young woman, scared and alone. He felt drawn to her as a man, more than as a preacher.

Darkness was claiming the sky and he hurriedly sought wood for a small fire. As the night grew he ate what was left of his food. He lay on the ground, his horse his only guard.

As he lay, he ran through his mind all the clearings he had slept in. His face was aged, his body hardened from his riding and sleeping on clearings like this. Even with that seasoning, he was inexperienced in the formal sense – buildings and pews and hymns. But he was well practiced in the ways of the wilderness, the mind of settlers, of Cane Ridge and the revival that was continuing. He nodded off under a cloudless sky, a direct path to heaven. He dreamed of her.

He arose early and rode into town. He nailed fliers to all the posts and walls. They announced the revival he had planned. Hear the Famous Robinson Manning preach! Bring your children! Be Saved! Be Baptized! See Miracles and Wonders! Healings and Deliverance!

Of the three buildings in town, Manning noticed a store. Harrison Supply was the name on the sign on the door. Flour bags stacked on the floor just inside the door – five high. Corn meal, too. Oats and wheat bags formed a path to the counter. His eyes followed that path. And there he saw her. Her face. The face from the creek. A soft beacon and a light of warmth. Her hair – a brown that glowed like the moon with the sun's help – hung over her shoulders. He introduced himself.

"Name is Robinson Manning, Methodist preacher from Connecticut."

A voice came from the back.

"Preacher, you bringing trouble?"

"Why, sir, would I give you trouble?" Manning said, eying the woman.

The voice came from a tall, bearded man wearing overalls who was now standing next to the woman behind the counter. He was older than her, older than Manning himself. Manning recognized him as one of the men who had stood in the street the day before.

"I heard about your kind. Anti-slavery preachers who come from New York or Boston and start trouble. I don't want trouble."

"I'm a preacher, come to share the word of..."

Then almost a chirp came from the woman, an excitement in her voice.

"You come to start a camp meeting?"

The man disapproved of the question with his eyes and went on speaking.

"We had a preacher come through here with them others. Sounded like you. About three months ago. On their way to Macon for a camp meeting – I'm sure you know them places – when you all preach together. Kentucky, I think. But that one, he was the only one who started talking about ending the way we live and freeing... Ran him from town. Sounded just like you... But I got my wife, here, Lucy, at that meeting. Guess it was good for something."

Manning saw the hope in the woman's eyes dim as surely as he felt it leave his heart. She belonged to another.

"No, I am not with any camp," he said as he slid one of his fliers from his bag. "I'll be preaching this afternoon down at that creek south of here. And stay a while to start a church."

"You plan to stay?" Lucy asked, hope returning to her eyes.

"Going to build a church here, right there on that creek after I baptize the first who are called to the Lord."

The man sent Lucy away, to the rear and slid the flier back to Manning. He wondered whether Lucy told her husband about the meeting the day before.

"Preacher, I built this store and I don't like trouble. I can sell you food for you and your horse. Supplies here are good. My wife here will make you some breakfast and feed you no charge. But we ain't coming to your preaching. We don't want no trouble."

Harrison cleaned the store while in the back Manning watch as Lucy prepared eggs and ham. He sat on a stool before a small table in a kitchen that was part of the living quarters.

He studied her. She was homely which made her virtuous. She wore a simple dress, another flower fabric with a white apron. She was not with child as he could tell. He felt drawn even more to her, like she was lost, in this village only for a short time, from somewhere else, a homebody, brought here by right not desire.

The food was quick and he ate as she made herself busy. She did not speak to him. He wished to inquire of her, about her. He wished to hear that hope in her voice. But to address another's wife was infidelity as it was to touch one. He ate and enjoyed, a preacher daunted by the will of God, tempted to change it.

He left and rode back to the creek. Along the way he saw no houses, no farming. Just woods. The crossroads sent roads north and to the west, the road he had taken here a year ago. Who would come and where would they come from?

At the creek, his horse watered. Manning sat along the bank and searched for a proper verse for his preaching that afternoon. Perhaps out of Exodus like he did in Alabama. The wilderness for the wilderness. Or the story of Paul's blindness, like he did in somewhere in Tennessee.

He had been so many places and preached to so many, even at his young age. He had been run from towns and escaped in darkness. He had not first come to free slaves, but free they would be with the word of the Lord. He had not come to start violence, but he had already seen it. In Carolina, in Alabama.

And he had not come to take a woman, but he had already thought on another man's wife.

It was that thought he tried to wash from his mind as he cupped water in his hands and splashed it on his face. He did not see his reflection in the troubled water – a sign, he thought, of his infidelity. I am a preacher, he said to himself. A preacher of righteousness.

Of all the places he had been and all the people he has saved, not one had been a woman like this.

He sat against the twin tree and fell asleep. He awoke at the sound of his horse licking water from the creek. They would be coming soon. The lost to the waters of life.

Something was needed. He stood up and knew he would need a pulpit. There he would place his Bible and then circle and circle it, standing on top of it – whatever the Spirit pushed him to. He looked around the small clearing and saw a boulder overturned down the creek. He went to it and pushed it upright. It was a rock in the form of a chair. But he did not sit in it. He saw it as a stepping stone. He would step up, his voice reaching higher to heaven. He rolled it from the water to the twin tree and waited.

He had no idea of the time and judged by the sun that it was well into the afternoon. The creek had an east and a west bank. He was on the east bank and when the crowd came and sat they would see the sun behind him, the aurora of light he remembered had appeared around the Lord. He stepped into his pulpit and raised his hands, like a man being pulled into the sky.

His eyes closed and the blackness was a canvas come alive. He could see gravestones surrounded by a metal fence. The fence was rusted. Vines grew over and among it. Tall oaks, ones that stood as columns in this mansion of woods, ones made to be, created for the purpose of marking this sacred ground. It was years into the future, 100 years, going on 200. In this place, this now old America, this now old land.

Beyond the fence, he could see more graves, lines and rows and open fields, hazy but certain. He wanted to see more, wanted to see what he thought was a fresh grave dug – what year was it over there? How long would the Lord labor here, by this creek? But his flight stopped at the fence. He stayed among those who were first called.

He knew who these people were. The stones marked the graves of all those who had died under his preaching here at the creek. All who had waded into the waters with him, all who had washed themselves and risen from the current. All who were living. His eyes surveyed the legacy and the inscriptions became clear. Our Precious Mother, it read. Our Beloved Father. A Child of Mercy. The names were missing, men and women and children and families and a community still unrecorded, to begin soon.

There was one name, one marker that was clear. Our Dearly Loved Preacher. Robinson Manning. 1804.

The canvas vanished and the blackness became dark, evil, death-colored. He heard screams, a woman shrieking, a woman crying. He heard the creek, the waters flowing, splashing, troubled. He was spinning, falling in the darkness. He finally saw light. It was then he fell from the stone, tripping into the water, the creek.

The sun beat the fading afternoon into his eyes. His feet were wet and his horse was startled. He stood, just off the bank in ankle-high water. He tried to bring his arms into the sky to collect more faith. But he could not. Instead he fell to his knees and covered his face with his hands. But the darkness, the canvas, the letters that became the words that became his death came again.

He was scared. His voice – the voice inside, the one he spoke to himself with, not the preacher's voice – announced the certain truth. I am to die soon. I am to die. Was the woman I heard her? And the creek, am I to be drowned? Am I to be shot? Who else but a sinful man would be given view of his death? He had no answer. But yes. Peter was given it. And Stephen, he died seeing Christ. Yes, the light. I saw the Lord, through the creek, the darkness, the falling, the light.

When would he die? He had seen his death but still there was time. There was time. The graves and the oaks. A church, with a line of faithful that seemed to go on 200 years. Yes. The Lord is willing to keep me here until I have finished my work. The Lord will protect me a little while longer.

They are coming, he thought. Those that shall be his church. Let them who have ears hear. He sat on the bank, his feet in the water. They would come. He would wait.

The silence turned him sleepy. I must be awake when they come. I must. He bent over and splashed water on his face. But moments later his head hung between his knees. How long had passed he did not know when he was aroused again by a bird off in the distance. The sun was lower, much lower. If he began now, if the Lord brought them now, he would have an hour. Let them who have ears come and be baptized.

He waded again into the water, this time knee high. Then step by step, sand on his feet, he waded until the water curled into his belly button. He put his hands on an imaginary backside and an imaginary head – perhaps her head, that hair – and dunked her into the water. He plunged his hands into the water and quickly brought her body, her clean body out of the water. She vanished as she came up. And he was left with his own thoughts, thoughts freed from holiness, thoughts centered on another man's wife.

He fell to his knees in the water, the creek nearly to his chin. My body clean and holy. Yet my head, my mind, my undoing. He closed his eyes and dunked his head, a bath that hoped to clean so much.

When he came up, with the water in his eyes, he saw her. Her face, her eyes meeting his. I still am unclean. He closed his eyes, to banish the picture to the blackness. He rubbed his eyes clear of water, as if to erase the vision.

He opened them and she was there. She poked out from behind the horse, her face, her arms, her body standing before him, her hand blocking the setting sun from her eyes. She stood there silent, as if she were embarrassed, ashamed.

As he walked out of the creek to her, he saw no horse and no husband. He did see she had brought a bag that seemed to be filled with clothes. Yes, he thought, she has come to clean again. The silence that grew as he walked to her was so strong that it choked his words as he stood dripping in front of her.

He did not know how to address her – this woman, this wife, this child of the Lord, this sheep he had just danced with in the water. Had she seen? What had she seen? How long has she been hiding behind my horse?

"Am I too late?" she asked. The voice, the hope it had returned.

His voice, the voice of the preacher returned.

"No, you are the first to come."

The preacher voice asked about her husband, but from inside came the answer, memorized words of the Lord: It is right, you have no husband. It was a wish bounded up in holy words.

"He does not know I have come."

He turned from her and patted his horse. He backed the animal from the creek and she followed, walking to his side.

"How did you come?" he asked.

"It is only a short walk."

He did not want to look at her face. He did not want to hear that voice. The voice that calls him outside. The voice of the strange woman who in the twilight of the evening lies in wait. I have come forth to meet thee, the harlot says, and I have diligently sought your face. And I have found thee.

He heard the harlot in his mind: My husband is not at home; he is gone on a long journey.

"I have come to hear you preach. I have come to hear you."

He heard the harlot again, with much fair speech, with the flattering of her lips.

"Will you take me into the water and baptize me?"

She is now with subtlety of heart. I have come to give peace offerings. I have come with fine linens and I have perfumed my body. I have come to break my vows.

And she caught him and kissed him. She held his face as she pressed her lips to his. He pulled back, she pulled forward, and then finally released him.

I cannot, he said softly. Was that in his mind? Or only in his voice? He did not know. He looked at her face and saw into her eyes. This sheep was no harlot. She was lost, taken from her home, by right and came here, came to this creek, by desire.

She looked at him and he saw her gazing. She was looking for hope, for the word of the Lord to save her. She was looking for cleansing. And the spirit led him to speak.

"Are you ready to proclaim your faithfulness?"

She nodded. He took by her hand and she led him into the water. Knee high and step by step until the water soaked the top of her apron. He stopped her there and floated his hand on the surface of the creek. He cupped his hand just below the surface and sprinkled water over her head. She closed her eyes as it fell past her chin.

Are you prepared to receive the Lord's cleansing?

Yes, my lord. Cleanse me from all unrighteousness. Save me.

Are you ready to enter new life?

Yes, my lord. Take me into new life. Take me away from here.

He could feel behind him the sun bedding its last rays of day. He could feel the warm water surrounding them. The angel of light stared into his eyes as he placed his hand on the back of her head and the other around her waist. She closed her eyes, in his trust. The creek swallowed her, the tomb held her. She was safe in his arms as the waters became clean around her, as she became clean by the waters.

And with his strength of the Lord he lifted her from the waters, breaking the surface of the water, breaking the hold of death on her, now alive and sealed for eternity.

And lo, the heavens opened and he saw her, the dove, colors dancing on her face in droplets of water.

A voice came from the wilderness and the water froze them, locked in each other's arms. Off his horse, storming from the ground into the waters, he was the only thing the preacher could see. She struggled to move but the depth of the water made her stumble and fall into the current. He bent down to grab her and the man was upon him.

The blade was high over his head and the preacher saw his death come. Again and again. He had no thoughts then but of the cemetery. Had he given up all that for the harlot? He goeth after her straightway, as an ox goeth to the slaughter till an arrow strike through his liver – as a bird hasteneth to the snare, and knoweth not that it *is* for his life. Let them who have ears hear.

The waters became bloodied as he tried to hold onto her. His grip faltered and his corpse sank into the creek.

Chapter Five

AFTER I TOLD RICK ABOUT the girls, he asked what I wanted to do. I told him I wanted to tell whoever needed to be told. He went and told Lovell and they both came back.

"You know where them girls at?" Lovell asked.

"Yeah."

I could hear Carey move in his cell, move closer to mine.

"Sergeant Patterson I think we ought to get him before a judge, a sheriff, somebody," Rick said.

"I don't think he'll get to go out... but he needs to tell me where they are at. I can make sure the right person knows. The warden can make sure. Wayne, do you know exactly where they are at?"

Then Carey shouted.

"Don't tell 'em. Don't tell..."

Lovell banged his stick on Carey's door. "Quiet!"

"Wayne, tell me what you know."

I stood there in the middle of my cell, arms at my side, looking through those bars at those two people – Hawaiian shirt and uniform. White and black. And I wanted to make it right. I did. But it wasn't ever going to be right unless I made it right with Momma. I guess Rick thought I was still deciding so he said something.

"Wayne we talked about making it right with yourself. Tell the sergeant what you know."

And Lovell added something, too.

"Wayne, this isn't snitching. He's dead and gone. This is about what the reverend said – making it right. With yourself."

Making it right with myself meant being sorry for what I did. I was sorry for what I did to Mr. Cho and his wife. But I wasn't sorry for what I did to Daddy. And it seemed I had to do a lot more than tell Lovell about the girls to make it right with myself.

I knew if I just told them then that would be the end of it. It didn't seem like that would be enough, for all that I knew, for all that I done.

Carey always said never confess before talking to your lawyer.

41

"I want to talk to my lawyer."

That night Carey started in on me as soon as the lights went out.

"There you go. Telling all your tales."

"This isn't my tale. He killed them girls."

"Why you telling them all this? I heard what they said about making it right. Shit, Wayne. Lovell don't care about that. This is about him getting good with the warden. The reverend – yeah – maybe he care about what's right. But he ain't nobody to nobody. You can tell him stuff. But changing like this – telling them all this – it ain't right. Them girls are dead. Dead. And in five days, you gonna be dead. After that it don't matter. What does matter is what you get out of this. And what you gonna get? Some more time in the yard? Some better service around here? Shit, Wayne. You ain't gonna get nothing. Nothing, shit nothing. And nobody wants shit."

Carey did always have a way with words. But he didn't change my mind.

That night he came back. He was walking back to that truck, from that graveyard. But when he got into the truck, he was gone. It was me in his clothes, looking at his hand touching the rearview mirror. I twisted it so he could see his face – my face – better. I looked into the mirror, looked at me as if I was in the mirror. He smiled, like he was enjoying it, like I had enjoyed it.

I woke up then. Lovell sometimes keeps the metal door open at nights because it gets so hot. He was walking by when I woke up.

"Bad dream?"

"Yeah."

He was about to keep walking but I stopped him. I had sat up in my bed with my feet on the floor.

"You ever dream bad thoughts? Like stuff you would never do. But still you see yourself doing it?"

"It's just a bad dream, Wayne. You done all the bad you're gonna do."

I laughed. He kept walking and I laid back down. Lovell was right – I had done all that I was going to do. Now, I was going to do something different.

The next morning – Tuesday – they brought my lawyer in. Lovell had told him that I knew something about some girls. They sat us down in the room where I was meeting with the reporter. My lawyer told me about my appeals – the typical ones, he said, and that he didn't think they would work.

And then he started listing all the stuff that I could get for telling what I knew. I knew I wasn't going to get out of the chair – and I didn't want that anyway.

"Maybe we can get you some more time with your family. They coming on Saturday?"

"Not yet."

"Maybe we can get you some time outside in the yard. You got Thursday coming. Maybe we can get you some time on Friday."

I sat there thinking – of all things – what Carey would do. I know he didn't want me to tell. But I bet if he had the chance to get something, to go somewhere, to get more time, he would tell.

I wanted to see Momma. And I wanted to make it right. To do that, I had to do a little wrong. Do a little for me. But it wasn't evil wrong. It was a small wrong – to trade some dead bodies for a trip to a graveyard. But Momma would be proud.

When I told my lawyer what I wanted, he looked at me for a long while. He knew about how she died and how I got caught going back to her. He didn't know about Daddy.

"That's what you want?"

"Yeah."

He looked off in the distance for a second or two, rubbing his chin.

"We can do that. Yeah. Get you before a judge. And tell him you know where some dead girls' bodies are and tell him we have a request. Yeah. We can do that."

Lovell rode shotgun. And the other shotguns came along too. That's what I remember about the trip to the courthouse in Jackson on Wednesday. My lawyer said I would only tell a judge about what I knew. Lovell wasn't happy. He wasn't disappointed, just mad that he had to take me to the courthouse.

My lawyer never gets to ride with me but he gave me a legal pad so I could write down all that I knew about the bodies. "Draw them a map if you can't think of anything else," he said when he handed it to me.

I was never good for drawing, though. I tried drawing the roads I knew he talked about but my lines were crooked because of the chains. I started to write my name and when I got to Michael I wondered if my son took my name.

He might not be a Mathis anymore, I suppose. But he's like me, like my daddy, like all the others. I was changing, though. Maybe you have to see yourself – like in a mirror – see yourself as evil before you can change.

Sometimes I see him at night. I'll be lying in my cell and I will dream about him. I don't know what he looks like so a lot of the times I see me – me as a kid – sitting at the table, talking to me now, like I was a real father.

I tell him all that I know, all that Momma told me. In my dream it seems like nothing has happened yet, that he hasn't done anything yet. That I haven't.

That's how the letter started.

My name is Wayne. I am your father. I am writing because on Saturday I will be executed here in Jackson. I was hoping that your momma would bring you. I am allowed to talk to my family for a few minutes before they take me. If you don't come I will understand. But there are some things I want to say here in case you don't come.

I didn't get very far in the letter because the trip to the courthouse was short. When I got off the van, I handed Lovell my legal pad. Read it, I said. While they were searching me, he looked it over.

"It's good, Wayne."

Because I am on the row, everywhere I go Lovell has to go. So he walks me in like all the other prisoners, through the back, and my lawyer was there waiting. He told me the judge's name, not to slouch, to say sir, and to let him do the talking.

I was brought into the courtroom and had to wait in the empty jury box while another case was happening. Lovell sat right beside me.

Your momma might have told you who I am. But she might have not told you what I am. I am a killer. I shot a gas station owner and his wife after I took their money. I don't know what else she has told you, but I have done some other stuff, too.

It is hard for me to write to someone who I have never known. I was there when you were born. But I had to leave a few weeks later. You used to live in my own house, even slept in my old room.

It's funny the stuff that pops into your mind – especially during the strangest times. I noticed across the courtroom a door open. But nobody came through it. Then there I was, in my room, in my bed. It was dark, and I looked up at the door and it opened but nobody was there. I remember that time because it was when I was a kid and I was trying to stay awake to listen for his truck. And I fell asleep and I heard something and then I looked at the doorway. The empty doorway.

I used to dream about sitting on the front porch with you. Like we were a real family. You would ask about Momma's church across the road. My momma always wanted to take me to church. I never went. I guess now I am telling you to go. You see, when people get going to church a lot, they start to change. They start to act differently and say things that most people wouldn't say – like thank you and I'm sorry. Rick told me that one time – that God teaches you how to say I'm sorry.

I'm sorry for killing those two people. I want you to know that. I tried and tried and tried to not kill anybody.

Lovell nudged me and walked me to the table where my lawyer was sitting. After the judge came back in, he told the judge why I was here. He didn't mention anything about what I wanted. The judge asked me if what I was hearing was true. I nodded and said yes sir. The judge said he needed to get some people on the phone and I stopped listening then and sat down. I handed Lovell my note pad again.

"I know, Wayne, I know."

I had always wanted to take you through the backyard to the creek that runs through there. I played there as a kid. My momma always used to find me there. I spent a lot of time there – swimming and fishing and floating down it. When it would rain, sometimes when I was allowed outside then, I would sit right there at the creek and watch the rain hit it. It would make tiny circles, and then they would float away.

I remember when Momma first told me about the creek. It was raining that day – it had rained a lot the days before. I was still small and because it was raining I couldn't go outside. Daddy had left that morning. The wind kept throwing twigs and bushes against the windows. Momma opened the door to let the dog in and we had to push hard as we could to close it.

It was then I saw her face. I put my fingers on her cheek – felt the blue and the black and a little red. Momma, what happened to your face? On the other cheek, Momma started to cry.

She knelt down and I could see right into her eyes.

Wayne, you're too young to understand some things. But you're old enough to hear this.

Thunder came and then lightening. I remember grabbing on to her.

Fight it, Wayne. Fight it.

Another thunder clap.

Fight what Momma? I'm scared. Fight what Momma?

Lightening. Rain coming down harder.

Fight what's in you, son. Fight what's in you.

What's in me Momma? I'm scared.

The creek – like your daddy and his daddy and all their daddies. The creek – living around here all this time and the creek's in you. Murder Creek has swallowed this family. Fight it, Wayne. Fight it, son. Fight it.

Wherever you are, whoever you are, whatever you are, you are like me. You got the creek in you. Your momma's a good woman and your grandparents and all the people you know are good, too. But I gave you this, I put the creek in you. My momma said I had the creek in me and I was supposed to fight it. I didn't. I couldn't. I didn't keep my promise. But you can. You can.

The judge finally came back in the courtroom. He made everybody stand and then back down.

"Mr. Mathis, I understand that you have some information for us. You will see that I have brought the prosecutor. And on the phone I have the director of the state bureau of investigation. And of course your lawyer is present. Tell us what you know."

I stood.

"I know where two bodies are buried – two little girls. That no one knows about me except me and the guy who killed them."

"And who is that?"

"Nathaniel Hollis. He was killed in..."

"Tennessee. Yes. Last week. And how did you come to this information?"

"He told me."

"Where?"

"He was in my cell."

"When?"

"When I was first in prison and he was too."

It was then my lawyer stood.

"Your honor, Mr. Mathis is giving this court some important information. And he is set to be executed on Saturday. He is doing it out of a changed heart, a remorseful heart. He understands the state's punishment for his crime and has no desire to trade what I am sure is well-received news for the family of these girls for any commutation. But he does have one request for this court."

"And what is that, Mr. Mathis?"

"I would like to see my momma."

"I am sure we can arrange for her to come..."

"She's dead, your honor. Mr. Mathis' mother is dead. She's been lying in a cemetery across the highway from his house for many years."

After I killed Daddy, I went back to Momma's body. She was lying on the floor in the hallway. I picked her up and put her in the bathtub. I tried to wash the blood off her face and get it out of her hair. What I could get out went down the drain. It was like she lying in a red pool.

She was all wet so I picked her up and put her on her bed and wrapped her in the big blanket she always kept there. I wrapped her head in some towels because her head couldn't hold her brain anymore. I found a comb and tried to make her look pretty but the comb kept getting caught in what was coming out of Momma's head.

When I had her in the blanket and with the towel around her head, I could still see her face. I put my fingers on her cheek – touching the blue, the black and a little red. I wiped my nose and sniffled.

I knew it would be getting dark soon. I left her in her bed. I found a shovel and walked across the highway. There was no sunset that day, none I could see. It was dark.

I found a clear spot and started to dig. Fight it, Wayne. Fight it, son. That's what she was saying – that's what I was hearing, her voice crying, telling me – as I pulled shovel after shovel of dirt from the ground. I dug deeper and deeper and harder and harder and it began to rain. The ground was getting muddier and muddier and it was hard to tell what I was digging into. But eventually I had a hole filled with water.

I walked back in the rain to the house. I went to the bedroom and loaded Momma under my arms. With the blanket and the towels holding her in my arms I carried her through the hallway, through the front door and outside.

The rain soaked the blanket and it became heavier and heavier. The rain dripped from my hair and made me stumble. But I did not drop her. Fight it, Wayne. Fight it, son. I carried her across the highway in the dark darkness to her grave. It was dark, but by the time I had got the cemetery it had stopped raining.

When I got there, I set the blanket roll beside her grave. I unrolled her and tossed the blanket aside. I wiped her face and smoothed her hair. Then from my knees, I scooped her into my arms and gently lowered in the watery hole.

She did not sink. She stayed on the water's surface. So I put my hands on her stomach and pushed. I pushed Momma into that hole until the water was up to my shoulders. It was the dirtiest water I had ever seen. Like the creek. I was pushing her body deep into it. I wanted to fall in, to be with Momma. Fight it, Wayne. Fight it, son. I let go.

But she popped up again. She came up and I could see her face and her hair and her neck. She was clean.

I wiped my eyes from the rain and there she was – floating at the top of her grave. I looked around for the shovel. I began to pile dirt – mostly mud, but some dry underneath – on top of her body. On her legs, then her stomach. And then I put a shovelful on her face. She began to sink as I covered her more and more.

"You want to be taken to your mother's grave before this state is set to execute you?"

"Yes, sir."

"That is not exactly an easy request."

I stood there not knowing what to say. My lawyer looked at me then he looked at the judge. I could tell he was thinking so I said something.

"I want to make it right, judge. I do. Them girls deserve to be buried right. But also I have to make it right with Momma. She never knew what I did – she died before I killed them people. And I'm sorry about that. I am. Ask Lo... Sergeant Patterson. He knows. And the preacher they sent to us. He knows. I want to make it right with Momma. I promise I won't be any trouble. She isn't that far away. Just down the road. At Murder Creek Baptist Church."

The judge looked at the prosecutor. He shrugged. He asked the man on the phone to say something. He didn't. The judge looked at my lawyer.

"A dying man's last request, your honor."

The judge was silent for a minute or two. He finally picked up his gavel and I knew what was coming next.

"Mr. Mathis, as long as the corrections department doesn't have any problems, I am going to grant this request. On two conditions. One, if one word of it, if one sentence gets in any newspaper before Saturday I will personally make sure they bury your body in a hole somewhere in the swamp. Two, you tell all that you know – names, places, trees, landmarks – and when they find the bodies I'll send word to the prison. Then you can go. You make this request. You live up to it."

I nodded and he banged his gavel. Lovell took me into a room with a table and some chairs. He left, but my lawyer sat beside me. Then the prosecutor came and he brought a tape recorder. He turned it on and I spoke into it. I told it just as he had told me – every detail, every dirt road, every turn. The way he put them in that old grave – right on top. The way he burned out of there. Even the way he smiled.

I came outside the room and Lovell was there. He walked me through the courthouse to the van.

I remember one evening – it was probably in the summer cause I was bored – I counted the graves. I knew Momma kept a listing of all the gravestones – it was her job as secretary of the church – and I asked her if I was right. She looked down at me and held my shoulders.

"Don't be playing in that cemetery. You might be stepping on some graves."

"But I counted 147. How many are there?"

"We don't really know. Probably a lot more. Sometimes stones roll over and get lost. Sometimes they buried them without any sign. Sometimes they buried people on top of other people. And who knows how far the cemetery goes. "

When I finished with Momma's grave, I walked around some and saw the names and dates. I made sure not to step on any graves. I started to think about all the people Momma said were killed by my kin. Were they all buried here? Is that how she knew? They rise like ghosts in a line and wander out over the creek, Momma said. Add one more to the line.

I picked up a stone that had turned over. It was so old I could hardly read it. It had broken off its bottom. I figured it was good enough so I stuck it in the ground, a half grave, for Momma. She deserved better, but I didn't know how to make it right.

I walked down to the creek. The creek runs behind the cemetery then under a bridge to our house. At the small clearing where boats can be put in, I walked into the water. I was wet from the rain and I guess I didn't care. It didn't seem like I was feeling the water. I got knee deep in the creek and for some reason, I stopped.

I stopped because I started to hear something. Momma wasn't saying anything now. It was Daddy, now. I was across the room on the floor, my knees in my stomach, watching him over her. He has beaten her with the tire iron and now had the gun in his hand. He bent down to her ear. Add one more to the line. That's what he whispered. I swear I heard it.

I know you probably won't be coming on Saturday. So I wanted to give you some advice, so you can do better than me. Always own up to what you do. My momma told me that and I am telling you that. It isn't always right what you do, but you can make it right by owning up to it. You can make it right for me.

You come from a long line of people who have done some bad things. But you can make it. You can make it right for yourself.

When Lovell came by Thursday morning, I was hoping he had the OK from the judge. He didn't. He did bring the warden with him. Lovell opened the metal door and the warden sat in a chair like Rick. But he was dressed in a suit with a tie. He said he was here to explain to me what was going to happen to me on Saturday. He had it all on a piece of paper for me to sign afterward.

First, the last meal. Nothing over $20. Nothing we can't get from around here.

Momma's cooking. Anything she makes.

Second, you'll have time with the preacher and your family, if they come.

He can make it right without me.

After midnight, we'll come get you and take you to the barber.

Momma with Daddy's electric razor. In the bathroom, in front of the mirror. I laugh when she finishes the first stroke down the middle.

Around 5 a.m. we'll start leading you to the holding room and then right before we'll take you in.

The death chamber.

The room will have the chair in it and some windows through which the witnesses and media can see you.

There they are. Right there. On the floor. He's holding on to her. She's crying and he's looking at her. And I am looking at them.

A microphone will be turned on for three minutes so you can make your last statement.

My voice. It's gone. They can't hear me. I'm sorry. I am.

After they have strapped you in the chair, they will place a black bag over your head.

In the darkness, will he come again? I'm scared, Momma.

Sergeant Patterson here will take a wet sponge and place it on your head. Then he will tighten the head strap over your hood. He will read to you the state's punishment.

My punishment. Cause I killed Daddy. Cause I am not sorry.

And then the electricity will be turned on. Do you have any questions?

Am I ready?

The warden left but Lovell said that I had some time in the yard. He led me down the hallway and through some doors until the one that goes outside. He opened it and I stepped into it, not knowing whether it was my final time outside.

When I get to go in the yard, they have to unshackle and unchain me. I am the only one allowed in the yard then. Sometimes I run along the fence. Sometimes I sit and smoke. But this morning I sat with my back to the prison wall and looked at Georgia.

I ran my hands through my hair. It wasn't too long. It needed a good shave. I rubbed my chin. That, too.

For all the studying me and Carey have done on capital punishment, we never read anything about the last time in the yard. Or the last time smoking. Or the last time seeing the sky by yourself.

Then the door opened. Lovell walked out and stood in front of me.

"They found them. Like you said. Right there."

I smiled.

"The judge said you could go tomorrow."

I smiled.

He smiled, too. I knew he didn't like it – cause he had to go, too. But he smiled all the same.

"Wayne, you did good. Real good."

I stopped smiling then and looked off past him. I was going over the execution in my mind.

"Lovell, you and me, we friends?"

"Yeah."

"You pulling the switch?"

"Nah. That ain't my job. They never tell me who does that. I'll be right there in the room... with you, Wayne."

"You're going to feel bad about it? About killing me?"

"Wayne, you done good here. About them girls. And Rick been telling me you talking to him. And that reporter you talked to him a lot. You did good. I'm sorry for you. But we all die."

"You think I'm evil? Cause I killed?"

"We all need to change, Wayne. Some more than others. We all need to change. You made it right, Wayne. For them girls."

I sat there for a second thinking about his brother. In prison somewhere, maybe looking out in the yard like me.

"Do you think your brother is sorry for all he's done?"

"I don't know. He's got some time to think about it."

"I've thought about it all my life... and... when I did it..."

I tried to tell him. I tried to tell him about Daddy. But I couldn't. I wanted to. I wanted to tell somebody that I killed him. I wanted to tell Lovell. I wanted to tell Rick. I wanted to tell somebody. Maybe they could help me feel sorry for what I did to Daddy. Maybe that would make it right.

"I know, Wayne. I know."

He really didn't know. But he said so all the same. Lovell was good to me.

"You thought about what you want for your last meal?"

I shook my head.

"You thought about what you gonna say?"

I started thinking about that black bag and not seeing Lovell's face but hearing his voice. I closed my eyes.

"Say something to the family, Wayne. Say what you said to your son."

I felt the water soak through the bag into my hair. It was cold. I felt the strap tighten and push the sponge into my skull. More water gushed out. It was dripping all over my face.

I opened my eyes.

"I'm not ready to die."

Lovell picked me up.

"I know, Wayne. I know."

When he walked me back into my cell, he said the reporter and Rick were coming by soon. I nodded. But before they came, he took me to the shower.

I took off my clothes and I stood there, alone, in the shower area. I have a little bar of soap they let you have and when I come out they give you a towel.

You only get 10 minutes. But today Lovell let me stay there longer. I washed my hair and all over and he still hadn't yelled for me. I looked at my hands as I stood under the faucet. I remember sticking my hand in the toilet for Rick.

I backed away from the faucet and let the water hit my hands. I stepped back into the flow. The water rushed past my face so much that I couldn't see. I covered my face with my hands.

It was cold water, cold like the water they use on the sponge. I wasn't ready to die. To see – to not see any more – inside the bag. I shivered under the water.

The water rushed over me more. I remembered what Momma said. It washed away stuff. That it was like starting over. The dirtiest water comes clean.

That's what she wanted. That's why she looked that way. When I finally came home that afternoon.

Everybody's head rose again after the amen and three boys dressed in all white, all wet in the water, stood next to the preacher in his white robe. I was the fourth boy, dressed in white, what was left of the white I was given, hiding behind a tree on the other side of the creek.

I saw Momma, standing alone. She was wearing her favorite summer dress – purple flowers and pink lines. And a hat. I wore those clothes – white shirt, white shorts, white socks that came up to my knees, and a new pair of white shoes – Sunday morning, letting everyone know that I was one of the ones ready to come clean.

Every day that week she told not to be missing on Sunday afternoon. When she came out yelling for me, I refused to move. Hidden under the front porch, covered in twigs, bushes, and a layer of dirt.

She yelled twice. Then she started walking. Walked the half-mile to the church with the creek running in the back and gathered with the others.

I waited there for the longest time. But I couldn't stay. Momma would be alone. I ran all the way through the woods, but I got there as the preacher was pouring the creek out of his hands onto the last boy's head. In the name of the

Father, the Son, and the Holy Ghost. Down you go, up you come. Amen. And you're clean.

She stood there, clapping like the rest of them, and I knew I had disappointed her. I know that face now.

She made her way from the creek and everybody else left, too. But I stayed. I crept out of the woods to the water. I took off my shoes and dirty socks and tried to wade into the water. I would do it now. For Momma.

But the water was too cold. It was June but the cold rushed up my leg. It wouldn't let me – the creek wouldn't let me in. I looked at my shorts and shirt – covered in dirt. I had to make it right. For Momma. I took them off and plunged them into the water. I found a rock and laid them down on it. And scrubbed. Scrubbed them against that rock. Twisted and twisted them watching the dirty water squeeze out. I scrubbed and scrubbed them and dunked and dunked them in that creek. I finally put them back on, slapped on my shoes and socks, and ran back to the house.

She was kneeling next to the front porch, in that dress, looking. Looking for me.

I ran all the way into her and pushed her into the steps. She fell backwards and sat against them. And as she cried, I cried. The only time I cried.

I tried, Momma. I tried to get clean. I tried.

It was the last time she tried, too. It was the last time she tried to get the dirty water, the creek, to come clean on me.

Chapter Six 1854

THE LOUD, CLANGING bell frightened Willie. He looked as much as he could for the source of the sound. He tried to turn his feet but the chains were too heavy. And then the man – the white man with the gun – lifted that gun. Willie froze.

The bell rang a few times and then stopped and Willie saw all the slaves come out of small quarters in front of him. They seemed to be looking beyond him. He shifted his head and saw two slaved walking a limping third from the woods. Willie guessed him to be a runaway.

Out from the estate house came a man dressed in a white shirt, collared and buttoned, tucked into some tan pants. He was surely Willie's new owner, the preacher from Milledgeville. That's all Willie knew about him.

The two escorts stopped the limping man in front of the preacher. He spit in the limping man's face. Willie thought he might wipe it off but he saw the man's shackled wrists. The reverend pointed his finger in the man's face.

You gonna go picking. Couldn't find a wife, here? You gonna go picking.

That's what Willie heard.

Someone pushed Willie from the back. He hobbled quickly until he was standing next to the limping man.

Strip him, the preacher ordered. Someone took the cuffs from Willie's wrists and ankles and he worked the raggedy shirt from the man's body and then yanked at his pants.

You gonna go picking. Willie had never heard that before.

The reverend walked over and whispered in Willie's ear: Welcome to the Lord's justice.

The guard turned Willie around and he discovered two towers of pine planted in the ground. Between their tops was another piece of solid wood connected to the towers as if they were fence posts. Attached to the middle piece of wood was a large iron cleat from which hung a pulley.

The escorts unchained the runaway and tied his wrists together, using the rope from the pulley. Then they pushed his left foot up to his right knee and tied the toes down to their opposite leg. They pulled him into the air just a foot or two off the ground and tied the rope to the posts.

They pushed a little and he began to swing. As he did, the coarse rope dug into the thin skin on his wrists. Willie was eying those wrists when the reverend slapped the thinner edge of a strip of cowhide into Willie's hand and then a willow switch into his other. Willie knew what he was being ordered to do. A growing young man, still not finished, taken and then a year in Carolina – a year into America – and now the new property of a preacher from Georgia, Willie knew what he was. But he had never hit. He had never struck another slave.

Willie stood there, stood there too long, staring at the large man hanging from the towers. The switch was taken from him and lashed across his own back. There was no way out. Either beat or be beaten. He looked one last time into the eyes of those around him and saw nothing – no one he knew, no one he could name, no one who would give him food later if he beat one of their own, no hope.

As he beat the open backside of a man he did not know, back and forth from switch to hide, he heard the reverend preach for the first time.

You cannot escape the Lord's justice. The Lord's justice shall reign here as in heaven.

The cowhide dug into the willow's claw marks, a rake then a hoe. Blood ran down the man's spine like water in a culvert. The man twisted and his body – back and stomach – remaining open to the enthusiasm of the reverend's justice.

Willie continued swinging that cowhide, his energy – or was it enthusiasm? – now matching the reverend's. A cadence developed, the preacher's words echoed by Willie's blows, then the horror of the man's screams, his groans between lashes. It was the climax of a great sermon. Willie pounded the skin like a preacher at the pulpit while the reverend's voice matched his rhythm.

The Lord demands justice. Switch. The Lord shall not be mocked. Hide.

Willie gave out after so many strokes. When he found the frenzy had faded from his face, he saw the result – red-stained soil, blood that oozed like mud. Groans – or perhaps one long moan – became the only sound the man could utter.

Willie thought it was over. But as he stepped back, someone drew a knife and sharpened the already pointed end of an oak stake and pounded it in the ground just under the man's foot.

The sermon continued. The Lord loves his justice and he loves his mercy, too. That's why the Lord loves his picking.

The reverend demanded more from Willie. He started again, pounding the man's calves and thighs. He turned to hit him sideways, sending the man swinging. Willie pushed the body away so he could swing harder. In a rage, he shuffled around the body, switch and then hide, switch then hide, like he was clearing heavy jungle with two words. For a moment he dropped the switch and closed his eyes. He swung the hide, using both sides, as if he were punishing himself. He swung as if he were beating himself, a conscious violently reacting to the violence its body was performing.

The hide stuck once in blood on the skin, slipping through its glue slowly, and Willie lost his balance and fell to the ground. Willie opened his eyes to the horror of sitting in the man's blood. More was now dripping from the sole of his right foot, the stained stake becoming Willie's third weapon. The man stood there on the stake, his face showing the agony of the mercy offered him: he could stop twisting, stop the dizzy spin of pain by resting his foot on the spike.

The Lord extends his mercy. But it meets his justice at the picket. The reverend finished his sermon and the punishment by grabbing the bent knee and spinning the man around like a top on the stake.

Willie watched it all, heard it all, done it all, his first picking, his first day, his first Sabbath in middle Georgia.

Lookie went inside after the picking to talk to the preacher. He had come dressed as well as he could – thin suspenders and a hat, but no jacket. He flattened his shirt with his hands and corrected his hat. He wiped a spitted hand over his hair. The reverend washed his hands with a wet rag held by a house girl and walked inside.

Lookie stood in the foyer and saw the large staircase and the chandelier above him. He saw the mud on his shoes – his only pair of shoes – and regretted walking along the creek to the house.

He followed the preacher into a room off the door – a sitting room with a fireplace, shelves filled with books Lookie couldn't read, and another chandelier. The preacher took out a cigar from a box near the fireplace and lit it. Lookie looked on, his hat in his hand. He knew not to speak first.

"You coming to the baptism?"

"Yes sir."

"Your slaves working out well?"

"Two fine workers you sent. Gonna have a good crop this summer."

"That dumb boy married himself a girl over on Reynolds' place. Went to see her last night. I sent two to get him and now look at him – worthless for weeks. Best worker, too. A lady told me that she thinks I treat them just about as well as it's ever worthwhile to treat 'em. And look what they go and do."

Lookie peered out at the window, but the curtains hid his view. He saw three or four black figures.

"You gonna make good on my land, Lookie?"

"Yes, preacher. Them acres you gave me are good acres. You gonna get good money."

He paused and stood up straight and tried his best to sound worthy.

"Mr. Browning I come to ask about... I've been going to your church now for some time and... I come to ask if you would marry me and... Eloise Jackson."

He watched the preacher blow smoke from his mouth, hoping each exhale included words. He let out three puffs before he threw the butt in the fireplace.

"Nasty ole thing. Made by some third-rate Jamaican someplace."

Lookie didn't know if he should affirm or keep silent. He started babbling.

"I've been doing good – two harvests now – on that land you let me work. And been coming to your preaching every Sunday. Even got baptized right after Eloise. She's a pretty girl. Her momma and daddy are dead and you been like a father to her and..."

He went through the negatives in his mind as he watched the preacher look out the window at his estate. This was not the first time he had asked. Six months ago as now, the preacher was right: Lookie didn't own land, didn't have any name, and didn't have any future. Yet.

Added, too, the preacher knew what Lookie did for his money. The preacher even bought from him, not asking any questions, taking a female just last month. But with the stealing he had done for others, and the ones he stole and sold himself, he had some money.

"You done good with the land, it being just you and all."

Lookie nodded. It was the same words he heard the first time.

"And you treat my slave property well."

Another nod. More repetition.

Lookie knew what was coming next. He heard it in his mind. A drunk father who bedded a traveling whore who died giving birth to an illiterate, illegitimate sharecropper who washed the shirt on his back in a dirty creek where his family has lived since before he was born. And a grandfather who destroyed the family name and future, killing a preacher of all things.

"The iniquity of the father, Lookie. You know that verse?"

"No, sir."

"I, the Lord thy God, am a jealous God, visiting the iniquity of the fathers upon the children unto the third and fourth generations."

Lookie stood silent, eying a portrait behind the preacher. Sitting on a chair in a jacket and full beard, the grandfather, the patriarch, once a preacher in North Carolina.

"You know the word iniquity, Lookie?"

"No sir."

"It means evilness. It means your grandfather and father passed on to you something that the Lord doesn't like. I believe in mercy and it's why I let you work that land. It's good land. It's good for you. But the Lord is jealous over his flock and I must be as well."

Lookie tightened the grip on his hat and tried to breathe a hundred years of the house in which he stood into his lungs. A breath of life for his family name. His chest grew but exhaled as the preacher stood face to face with him.

"This is the last time I want you here asking about her. I got a cleansing."

The preacher left the room as Lookie took a last breath of a house, a life, name that exhaled quickly because it wouldn't stay in his ruined lungs.

When the justice was done, the watchers scattered. A house girl brought Willie a bucket and pointed him to the creek. As he was leaving he saw an old man lift the limping man off the ground.

The creek was only a short walk and there he knelt beside the water to fill the bucket. He saw the water slowly come by, leaves and sticks taken downstream. He could jump in, wade across, run. He could wade down the current for miles. He could escape, live free, somewhere, anywhere. Anywhere where there was no picking.

He could. He would, except he didn't know where the waters went or how far was the next town, the nearest train, free land. He barely knew north from south, catching the sun over his head. And he was most afraid from the start of how far the Lord's justice could extend.

When he returned from the creek he found the runaway and set the bucket down next to him. Then he cupped water onto his back. "It'd be alright."

Willie started to rub his fingers lightly over the welts. Deep gashes, bloody divides between the edges of the ridges. They lined his back in all directions.

An old man started to sing. The Lawd lays his cross on us all. He went to dat cross for us all.

Willie noticed the water making mud on the floor. Then he felt someone grab his hand, squeezing Willie's fingers.

He be ready soon. To drown you.

Willie tried to take his hand away but the beaten slave refused. His eyes held Willie as much as his hand.

When he drown you, don't come up. You want to be free? Stay in dat water.

The old man continued to sing. Good day for the Lord's drowning. Good day for a drowning man to be saved.

Willie raced through his memory. On the ship that brought him over, black face upon black face, the whites of the eyes showing there was another body next to you. You could hear the ocean ram against the boards. Sometimes water seeped between and wetted his back. Groping for anything, touching something, smell the dominating sense. Death held much of the room inside the hull.

And then the door opened – light into the darkness of days – and Willie could see bodies being pulled out from the room. Then Willie was pulled out with the others near the door and stood on the deck as the white men tossed bodies overboard.

They all sank except one. When the water hit him he started to struggle, even cough. He screamed in a foreign tongue and flailed his arms, trying to near the ship. Two men argued on deck and pointed at the man drowning. Willie watched as the man wailed and tried to remain above water. The waves hid his head, drowning him for a few seconds, and then it reappeared. The water splashed in his face and made his words even less intelligible.

Drowning man alive. Drowning man alive, someone yelled. A rope thrown into the water, but too far away. The waves taking him down for longer and longer. Drowning man going down.

His arms stopped, his shoulders waded for a second or two, and then his black-haired head sank. Drowning man drowned. Willie was shuffled back into the darkness.

Lookie didn't want to go to the creek. He was angry, proud angry, angry enough to beat. But she had wanted him to come. There will be picnics and dancing after the baptism, she said.

Baptism always happened when the preacher had new arrivals. That first Sunday after he bought new slaves, he brought the whole church to the creek and washed them in the water. Lookie had taken from of them before. The new arrivals are the best ones to get. The shock of it all – a new place, a new master, a longing for where they'd come from and where they lived before that – all that was racing through their minds those first few nights.

Lookie had always figured if someone were going to steal from the preacher, the best night to try was Sunday night – seeing how the preacher gives them the day off. And after baptisms, there was usually dancing well into the night and it would be easy for someone to slip onto the estate and get away with a slave tied to him. There was no better time.

He had never stolen from the preacher. Never tried.

By the time he got to the creek, there was already a large crowd. Lookie waded through them, trying to find a spot to see the water best. And then he looked for her as he hugged a tree.

The preacher had a new arrival dressed in white as frightened as an animal. Lookie found himself judging him as a prize, as something he would steal. He noticed the slave was shorter than the preacher, but looked strong in the shoulders. No marks on his face or chest, either.

There were two rules for this business. One: Never steal the branded – one missing an ear, having a long, obvious scar or something that made him different. He might be recognized as owned. And two: Never get caught with one. Ever. It was a capital offense, like horse stealing. And the preacher was high on the Lord's justice.

He had never stolen from the preacher. Never wanted to.

Through the crowd he saw her. Dressed in a white dress with a black sash around her waist, she wore a flat hat with flowers in the top. He waved with a flick of his hand and she smiled. She knew nothing of the preacher's rejections. He kept the first one from her because he was ashamed. Tried to make himself better after that. Now, angry and seeing that slave there strong and clean, he felt his shame grow into pride. Just to see if he could, he would. Make some money, maybe even steal it back.

He had never stolen from the preacher. Now he wanted to.

A pathway through the people was made as Willie stepped into the water and his feet touched the sandy bottom. His toes dug in with each step toward the middle.

The reverend's voice boomed throughout the crowd.

Here in these waters a holy man – a preacher like myself – was killed. It is why it is called Murder Creek. And all who come out of it, all who are buried with the Lord, all who are baptized in this holy water, will be clean. All who are clean are free.

Willie's foot sank in the sand as he tried to turn and go back to the bank. The preacher grabbed him by the shoulder. He whispered in Willie's ear.

Welcome to the Lord's mercy.

He raised his right hand and put it on Willie's forehead. Then Willie was pulled backwards into the water. He quickly closed his eyes as the water surrounded him. His last sight was the cloudless sky above him turning brown.

The water swallowed him, taking away his breath like the closing of a crypt. He coming to drown you. You want free? Your life for freedom.

He tried to find the bottom and his knees buckled and he fell backward. He felt free for a few seconds. He sloshed around for something to hold onto. His hands slid off rocks and drowned limbs. He kicked and squirmed. But soon the mighty hand of the master dragged him above the water.

Willie heard singing. The Lord saves a drowning man. The Lord saves a drowning man.

He saw the preacher's eyes and Willie knew he would hear that bell soon.

Lookie found Eloise dancing in a circle of women after the baptism. He grabbed her out of the whirl and rushed her against the tree and kissed her. His face remained just over hers as he whispered lies to her.

"You're gonna marry me soon."

"When?" she asked.

"This week."

"Where?

"Here."

The preacher was wrong. He was a preacher, not a prophet. He would marry. He would sell the new arrival, come back and take Eloise to the nearest preacher he did not know, return here to this creek and live – iniquity be damned. Himself, too. His sons, too. If the preacher was right on something. And on and on down the line, damn them all with this love.

"Have my son."

She smiled.

She spun away from the tree, leaving his hands last, and walked near the bank. He walked behind her and hugged her. He held her tight, feeling the iniquity in himself, the purity in her. He pulled her close to him, trying to pull it into his own body.

He would have a family, a name. He would marry. He would take this slave, sell him off, steal him again, and tell the preacher he had found him his missing slave. The preacher would let him marry then.

As the afternoon grew old, the crowd at the creek thinned more and more. Lookie and his Eloise sat on the bank until the last bit of sunlight was left for her to make her way home.

They stood and kissed one more time. She took a path away from him as he headed back toward the preacher's estate.

It was near sunset when Willie heard the bell. He was dragged from his quarters and the crowd gathered with him under the twin towers. When the preacher came out and stood in front of him, he whispered.

It's time to buck up.

Someone pushed him to the bloody ground and grabbed his hands. They were tied and stuffed into his stomach. A coarse rope was run underneath his legs and Willie was taken through the air by the pulley on the picket. He hung upside down facing the preacher and the crowd of slaves, holding his arms to his chest, lest his fingers dip into the dried blood.

It's time to buck up.

Willie saw the preacher roll up his sleeves and grab the hide.

The Lord shall not be mocked. Willie curled up with the first slap to his back.

Buck up.

The preacher belted his stomach and Willie curled up again. The blows were measured for their power, slowly assessed for their effect and grew in intensity. After five hits Willie caught on. When he curled, or bucked, the next hit was harder. If he stayed straight, there was more time to rest. Another hit came. Willie tried to freeze his frame but the hide sent ripples through his skin that forced his body to cling to itself. Another hit came.

Soon mercifully Willie was lowered to the ground.

Another slave walked Willie back to a cabin and when they arrived Willie felt water on his back. He heard singing. The Lawd lays his cross on us all. He went to dat cross for us all.

As the water ran down Willie's back, he saw John's face and knew he had to leave. He had to run somewhere, nowhere, anywhere from the bucking.

Lookie watched, hidden, as the old man led the new arrival from his beating. Lookie knew by the way he walked, the way he could walk after that bucking, that he could make it across land. He saw freedom in his eyes. It was always hard to compel the right one to leave, but the ones that Lookie had stolen always had that look. They were more afraid of staying than getting caught.

Fires burned in the distance where the slaves made their own dancing after the baptism. Even in the darkness, Lookie stuck close to trees and walls. But he finally came to the first of the quarters. He peered inside and saw the three men sitting inside. They said nothing as he stepped in and pushed the door behind him.

One was lying on the floor, his face toward the wall. Lookie saw the scars and knew he was the one from the morning picking. An old man sat in the only chair. And then to the right of the door, he saw the one who took the bucking sitting with his knees in his stomach.

"You the new one?"

Willie lifted his head and nodded.

"You walk?"

He nodded.

"You run?"

Willie stood up and lifted his knees, one at a time, to show the white men he could do anything to be free.

"I can take you across the creek, down a bit. I got this guy waiting and he can take you on til you get where you want to go." It was the lie that set a thousand hearts free.

Willie nodded and Lookie turned to leave. A slave lunged forward and grabbed the young slave's hand. He was the one who had been singing. But his next words were not based in a melody. The Lawd lays his cross on us all. Can't run from him. He all around.

Willie shook free and was outside with Lookie. Lookie knew he needed something to tie himself to the slave, to make sure he didn't take off. He cut off some rope from the picket and tied Willie to his wrist. Then they set out toward the creek.

They began in rhythm their run and made their way to the creek. Lookie pulled the pair to cross it so they could run down the other bank. Willie paused for a second, testing the sandy bottom. Lookie tugged on the chain and pulls a stumbling Willie into the water. They trudge across and make their way onto dry land.

Listening to only the sounds of night – whatever bird was out, the slow rustle of dark wind, and the current pushing past – the free man and the freeing man ran in tandem.

It was a good half hour before Lookie started hearing things. He squatted when a deer crossed ahead of them. He turned at an owl's sound. And he thought he heard the sound of feet breaking the surface of the water behind him. He was growing paranoid, growing a conscious, that inside voice of the preacher telling him he wasn't going to succeed.

The danger sounds slowed their run to a walk and kept them immobile for periods of much needed time. Surely someone would discover them soon, someone would come looking. Lookie had always made it to the first stop before he heard any sounds. Now the sounds were more frequent, closing in on them.

Willie grew more afraid with each stopping. His legs and back ache but he does not stop, will not pause for pain. But every few yards he is dragged down to a squat.

The water was deep enough to run on their thighs. Willie saw the white man beside him and his thick legs and knew he could never run from his grip.

Within the next few minutes Lookie heard the barking of dogs. He knew the preacher had dogs. Dogs that could smell a runaway a hundred yards in the woods. Lookie jerked his prize into the water and walked near the bank. The splash of a shoeless slave and a booted sharecropper echoed each other.

Another dog bark raced to his ears and Lookie heard the muffled orders of the human behind it. He squatted in the water, knowing he is far from safety. This night fills his head with thoughts he never had before while stealing. If he keeps running, they keep following. If he keeps splashing, they keep coming. He could hide, but the dogs always win. The preacher was right – he wasn't a killer or a drunk but he was his father's son, his grandfather's name. They would shoot and he would die here, chained to a slave, another generation of iniquity.

He had taken lots of slaves, ran them free for a few hours. But he was never free, never able to shake what he could not ever shake. But this run – this slowly failing run – this was supposed to be his flight, his first flight to freedom.

Willie whispered something about drowning.

Lookie felt the water on his shins and scooped a handful. His water. The creek he would never leave. As he watched the water fall through his fingers, Willie tried to run. Lookie pulled on the chain and stared at him. Yes. He's better to me dead.

"It ain't me who gonna drown."

He punched Willie in the face, knocking him back into the water. Lookie jumped on top of him, punching him again in the face and then the stomach as the water got between his hands and their target. He grabbed the raggedy hair he saw poking out of the water and drew Willie's face up. His eyes had swelled, filled with surprise. He gasped for breath as his freedom slipped away, his soul locked in a new set of chains.

Lookie saw nothing but blackness. He shook it and plunged it back in the water.

The dirty water forced its way into Willie's mouth before he could close it. It clogged his nose and his ears. He felt the man on top of him, his grip on his head unmovable. Willie kicked and tried to squirm but he remained underwater, under the powerful man who had promised him freedom.

Lookie quickly began to use two hands with his legs squeezing the breath out of Willie. Both hands kept his face under the surface. Willie tried to bite but the water only filled his mouth. Willie bucked and kicked but the more he did the more water overcame his breathing in what was quickly becoming another drowning.

Lookie had to struggle less and so turned his head back and saw lanterns. He pulled the head down further into the water, tugging it back and forth. The kicking had stopped and he could feel the lungs filling up less. He dug the back of the head into the creek bottom and waited for death. Willie saw nothing but darkness. He could not tell if he was alive or dead, but he heard that old man singing. The Lawd saves a drowning man.

Quickly Lookie untied the rope and threw it down the creek and it floated away. He stood up and kicked his prize one last time. Nothing but a corpse. He ran to the other bank and squatted, hidden in the bush.

He jumped up and out into the water just as the dogs arrived. The preacher and two slaves were fifty feet behind them. As the dogs ran over the body and began barking at the corpse, Lookie pulled one away. He yelled to make sure the preacher heard him.

The preacher arrived, the slaves carrying each a lantern.

"Lookie you chasing my runner, too?"

"Yes, sir. Saw him run from the quarters and followed him down the creek. He's a sneaky one – lost him some time ago. But then I heard the dogs and caught sight of him. He didn't see me. But I guess he got the fear and drowned himself."

The preacher knelt down in the water and pulled the watered face from its grave.

"Weak. Just weak. Buck him and he runs."

Lookie's nervous sweat was hidden by the water on his body, the fear pumping his heart replaced by his running from the bank. He offered more evidence for his story.

"I chase him clear down this creek."

The preacher shook the lantern across the body one last time.

"This one was gonna replace that one I put through the picker this morning."

"I can get you one, preacher. Good worker. I can get you one. For free."

The lantern came back to Lookie's face.

"The Lord bless you," the preacher said as he smiled in the lantern's light. "Bless that new bride of yours."

Chapter Seven

AFTER I GOT BACK FROM the shower, I fell in my bed and began to count the hours I had left. It was past noon and Lovell had fed me. Hamburger and fries. Carey said he liked it, too. With Friday and the six hours on Saturday, I had 42 hours. Not even two days. I was going to see Momma but I wasn't ready.

I thought about all the people who died in Murder Creek – all the people my kin have killed – and wondered if they knew how much time they had before they died. Did they know they had five minutes or ten or did they not see it coming, did they not know they were going to die?

Lovell came and got me a few minutes later and said the reporter was here to see me. On the way, Lovell reminded me what the judge said – no news. I nodded.

We said hello and I sat down. Lovell stepped behind me.

"How you been?"

"Good."

I had been good, doing good. Telling about them girls and all. I wanted to tell him that, after remembering what I said when he was here before. Bang. Bang. Bang. Emptied the whole clip.

"You write that letter to your son?"

"Yeah. Thanks for the address. I thought you were coming sooner."

"Sorry about that – if I made it seem like I would come. I did want to come but I had some places to go."

"Like where?"

"I went down to read that historical marker. All about the Indians and the settlers. I went into the graveyard, thinking she may be there. But I didn't find a stone with her name on it."

"She's there. Just no stone."

"Who buried her there?"

"I did."

"And you couldn't get a stone?"

"Nope. But do you know what I did with the money – the money from the store? I tried to buy one. I went to some stone maker in Eatonton and he recognized me from the news. The police had given out the tape. That's how I got on the run."

He smiled a little bit. It was funny to me, too, now.

"I also talked with the lawyer who did your trial. He said he would be there on Saturday."

I nodded.

"He said that he thought you had a good chance of getting life because of your childhood. He said your father beat your mother."

I nodded again.

"Yeah, that's how she died."

"Did he beat on her a lot?"

"Yeah."

"When was the first time you remember?"

I ran when I saw him swing. I heard the slap after she called him a drunk. I guess he heard me run out the front door because when I looked back he was standing on the porch. I didn't know where I was going but I got across the highway to the church. I tried to pull open the doors but they were locked. I yanked and yanked but they did not move. I was so little my shoes slid toward the door as I tried to open it.

I guess since I was at a church I got on my knees. I faced the locked door, put my hands together like Momma said, and closed my eyes. But when I closed my eyes I saw him beating her. I saw his hand turned to a fist and he was punching her, right and left, holding onto her hair like her head was a bag. My eyes popped opened and I started to talk to the white door. It was like the door to heaven.

I asked God to put Momma in heaven right then, to save her from Daddy.

I ran back home to see what had happened and Daddy had left by then. Momma was in her bathroom, washing her face. She asked me where I had gone.

Momma, I prayed God would take you to heaven. I got on my knees in front of those white doors and asked God to save you.

She rubbed her hand on my head. My little angel. In heaven with me.

He might have been gone, but Momma wasn't safe. I didn't tell the reporter, but it was the last time I asked for something.

"Did she ever fight back?"

"That one time – that day when he killed her."

"You ever fight back?"

It was the first time I knew I could kill someone. It was the summer after I started high school. He had started in on her, beating her and I walked in on them. I ran and tackled him into the wall. I heard a deep groan when I backed away. He stayed down for the longest time. I thought he was dead.

I think that's when it first hit me of where I came from. That the creek was in me. I meant to put him out and as I stood there looking at him – it was just a minute or so – I thought I had killed. Momma put her hand over her mouth as if I did. Then he got up and gave me ten times what he did to Momma. All that summer I stayed away from him. Until he killed Momma I stayed away.

Right up until Momma died I started thinking more about all the stories she told me of my kin. I never really knew how many of the stories Momma told me were true and how many were just her stories. But all of them starting being all true to me then. I started to see what she meant. I started changing then.

"I talked to some people who live around Murder Creek. They said your father served time in prison."

"I turned out just like him. It's a long line."

"What was he in prison for?"

"Before he married Momma, he shot a man. He didn't die or nothing."

When Momma was in the hospital that time over Christmas she told me about Daddy serving time. Said he told her one night after he had been drinking that he lay there in his bunk as someone got stabbed. He laid there listening to the man die. He was young and scared and had to watch the stabbing, too. But after that, he stared straight at the ceiling in the bunk. Never once did he lean over and look. When he told her that, she said, he was stone sober. Quick as that – raging drunk, going on and on about prison and the fights and then he looked at her with some sort of new face and said he never wanted to hear those sounds again.

I never want you to see that, she said. No killing. No dying. I don't want you in no prison. Your daddy came out different. He came out like your granddaddy.

My granddaddy was dead before I was born. But Momma said he was mean and bitter all his life. I know that after you kill someone, you change. And after you watch someone die, you change, too. I did both. I watched that creek take him, take control from him. Then it took it from me.

"You ever seen someone die?" I asked.

The reporter took off his glasses and wiped them with a rag from his pocket. He shook his head no.

"When I watched my mother die, it was like she had something grabbed out of her body – all ghostlike. Do you think that's how it's going to be with me?"

"I don't know."

"You ever seen someone get executed?"

He nodded. "Once."

"What is it like to die? How do they look when they die?"

He put down his pen and swayed back a little.

"Sometimes it doesn't go well. They don't die as quickly as they're supposed to."

"Yeah I know that. But when they do – when they die – have you seen what they see?"

I think what I saw when I shot Mr. Cho and his wife was what them people who killed saw, what they had in them, the creek rising. The stories I heard – slave killings, preacher killings, family killings – the main characters were there at that store. Not ghosts, but doing what they did, doing what they did while I did what I did. We all killed and we all killed at the same time. That's the creek rising – rising from the Indians through the years to me.

The reporter didn't know what to say but he tried.

"You ever shock yourself accidentally? It's like that – only more and for longer time. What you feel in that finger is run through your whole body. And they can't see out of the bag they put over your face."

"I know what it's like. I know how it works. But how do they feel?"

I guess I was looking for something he didn't know. He shook his head as to say he didn't know. He came up with a response, though.

"They feel like they're dying and there is nothing they can do. I think that is what they feel."

"I think that's how Momma felt. But Rick – the preacher I been talking to – said Momma was ready to die. He said I'm not ready. He said I would know, though, after I make it right with everybody."

"How you going to do that?"

"I already started. Remember that man you told me about – the one who sang in Tennessee? He and I bunked together and he told me some stuff he never told anyone. I told a judge and they found some girls' bodies."

He started writing that down. Lovell walked up with a soda and stared at me. I nodded. I wasn't going to tell. Momma was more important. But he had to know – know I was changing. They had to know that I was changing.

Lovell stood there and I knew it was time to go.

I think the reporter didn't notice so he asked one more question.

"You say you making it right with everybody. Did your father ever make it right with you? Whatever happened to your father after he killed your mother? Did he ever..."

Lovell grabbed my arm.

"You going to be there on Saturday?"

"Yeah. Right here. Before you go."

"Ask me again, then."

I guess I was promising to tell him about Daddy. But I didn't really want to. Then they might not think I was changing. Even mentioning him makes the creek rise. But where he's at, he is making it right with me, though. Making it right for all that he did.

I went back to my cell and Rick was there waiting on me, trying to talk to Carey.

"Sergeant Patterson, this inmate does not want any counseling," Rick told Lovell as we walked up.

Carey was singing like a young boy. Squealing, really. Amazing Grace, I think. If I remember correctly.

Lovell put me back in and shut the metal bars, but not the solid door. Then he looked through the meal slot at Carey and left.

Rick had on that Hawaiian shirt again. It made me laugh again.

"You going to wear that on Saturday?"

He smiled and shook his head.

"You ever been to Hawaii?"

"I went there just a few weeks ago, before I started coming to talk with you. I didn't really want to go, to tell you the truth. I hate planes and I don't like to be out in the sun all that much. But we went and I started to like it. And then when we left, the people we stayed with said they saw me change so much there they gave me this shirt."

"You been changing me."

He smiled and shook his head again.

"No you been changing all on your own."

"Carey don't like you much." I banged on the wall next to me. Carey banged back. Rick smiled.

I hung my body on the bars in front of him, arms above my head. I was tugging on the immoveable bar. It was strange talking to the reporter. I started to wonder why I said all those things. He thought I wanted to talk to him so I could get my name out. I guess I just wanted to talk. Same thing with Rick. I want to tell someone, to have them hear.

"My momma always said you should own up to things you've done."

"Wise woman, your mother."

"Yeah. I sure got a lot of things to own up to."

"You figured out what you want to say on Saturday?"

"Yeah. A real good apology to that family. To everybody."

"You got something to say tomorrow, too?"

I back away from him and looked down at the floor and nodded. There was one difference talking to that reporter. He didn't make me look this way. I finally pulled my head up and looked at Rick.

"You know you said that when I went back to see Momma that I went back to tell her how sorry I was for becoming a killer. You were right. But I never made it to her grave. I jumped out of that car with that gun – like you said. But I paced and paced in that graveyard on the other side from her. I did go back to tell her, but I couldn't. I couldn't tell her I failed. Then she wouldn't be proud."

"Is that what you are going to tell her tomorrow?"

What I couldn't tell Momma was rising in me. I am pacing the cell as I paced in front of those broken stones, grass high to my knee. I hear myself talking aloud, waving the gun. I hear sirens. The car is still running, driven all the way up off the dirt road to the rusted fence. I take a step toward her. I have to tell her. No. I can't. I step back.

I stepped toward Rick.

"You ever don't feel sorry for something you done?"

He leaves me on the floor and heads to the kitchen, leaves her there, dead. I hear him drop a bottle on the floor and swear. He can't see me. I'm hidden.

"Yeah, sometimes. But over time it gets to me."

The gun is lying beside her. I crawl over and grab it.

"How long does it take?" I say as I grab the cell bars, back from the end of the cell.

I feel it in my hands. I grip the handle and rub my other hand over the barrel.

"It depends, I guess on what I did."

I look at Momma. It isn't her. Her hair, her face, her head – her. She's lost. I'm lost, lost to the rising creek. I stand up and now he sees me, sees the gun pointed at him.

I don't get too close cause he might try to wrestle it away. But he does anyway. He lunges at me and I step aside and hit him on the back of the head with the gun. He ends up on his knees in front of me.

You killed Momma, you bastard. Now I'm gonna kill you.

I wave the gun as to show him the way – the way outside, the way to the creek. I open the door for him and he walks through, either too drunk to grab for the gun or too scared. We walk down the porch, through the yard to the creek with me behind, gun never moved from his head.

"What is it, Wayne?"

Boy, whatcha you gonna do with that gun, boy? You ain't gonna shoot nobody, boy. Your Momma's dead but she left a little momma's boy – ain't ya?

He turns around, trying to scare me, but he sees the barrel and kept walking.

We come to the bank where the twin trees stand, where there is a boat landing. Walk in the water, I say, as I point the gun toward the creek. He gets to his shins and stops.

They came then – all those voices, all the people, those killers, those who died. They fought in my mind like they were trying to win me over. Them who killed were killing as they did and them who died were dying all over again.

I heard his feet shuffle in the water as if he was coming out. I fired. Bang, bang, bang. The whole clip.

Each release another tug on the cell bars. Each bullet from the gun another kick at the metal door. I finished firing and stood there in the silence.

"Can you ever make yourself feel sorry for something that you aren't?"

"That's what changing is, Wayne."

"Sometimes it helps to talk about it. Talk about it with God."

I keep seeing Momma on that floor. What was she seeing then? And right before then? When did she first see God?

"Rick, you ever seen a person die?"

"Like in here?"

"Any way."

He nodded.

"What do they look like when they die?"

"It depends I suppose on how they died."

"That reporter said when he saw someone get executed that they were afraid, that they looked like they had no control over it. Is that what you saw?"

"I think maybe he's right. I think most people who get executed aren't ready. The people I've seen die – my father, some people in a hospital, and even an old inmate – all seemed ready. They were not always willing but they understood where they were going was better than here."

"You mean heaven?"

"Yeah."

I closed my eyes. The white doors. I start to shake them. But they won't move. Yank and yank and yank and my fingers sliding off the handles and I hear the hinges and the wood cracking. But it's closed. It's closed to people who aren't sorry, who aren't clean. I'm sorry, Momma. I'm sorry for disappointing you. I'm not going to be in heaven with you.

Then there is a hand, two hands.

"Wayne. It's all right. Wayne, let go."

I open my eyes and Rick's still holding onto my hands. He waves off Lovell down the hall. He looks at me, looks at my eyes. He presses his hands down over mine.

"There's more than Mr. Cho and his wife, isn't there?"

I look down at the floor. I could feel my words slipping away because of the sniffling. I pulled away from him and sat on my bed, hands in my head. He stayed at the bars.

"Momma wanted me to do it. She wanted me to do it and I didn't. She wanted me to go into that creek. But the creek is in me. I had to become this. I had to become this. That's why I'm not ready. Won't ever be ready. Won't ever change."

"What did she want you to do?"

"Get baptized. Go into that creek – down and up and rise again. Like she said. She said it would clean me, wash away all that was in me. Make me the last in the line."

"Is that why you think you disappointed her – you never got baptized and you killed those people?"

I'm sorry because I didn't keep my promise.

She's covered in a sheet, her head in bandages, the wires sticking out of her. I lean on the bed rail and hold her hand.

Momma, I'm gonna get him. I'm gonna kill him.

Your daddy sorry for what he done – he loves you and he loves me. He sorry. Real sorry. Stay here, Wayne. Stay here. Promise me you won't go. Promise God you won't go. Promise me you won't go. Promise God, Wayne.

So I stayed. I stayed and she came home and he beat on her. And I didn't fight back. I waited. Until she couldn't make me promise anymore.

"Yeah I disappointed her. Cause I killed. Cause I'm not getting into heaven. Cause I'm not ready to die. Cause I'm not sorry."

I stood up in my anger and faced Rick at the cell bars.

"What aren't you sorry for, Wayne?"

I watched him fall backwards into the water. I ran into the water, firing an empty gun at a dead man. That bastard wasn't sorry.

The creek drove me to that store – where the voices came – and I stood there, hoping to feel sorry, to feel anything. I fired. Bang. Bang. Bang.

"She didn't know what she was saying. Those were the drugs talking. But she made me promise. Made me promise to God not to go. Made me promise not to kill him. And God – he knows I'm not sorry for doing it. But I promised. That bastard – he beat on her and beat on her and then he shot her. He shot her, making me watch. I killed him and I'm not sorry. But you see? I promised and... I promised... you see?"

For the first time in my life, I saw tears. I had felt them before – trying to wash those clothes, at Momma's hospital bed, and walking in that cemetery – but now I saw them – one after another, slowly but surely, the creek ran out of me. Down my cheeks.

I hunched over the cell bar, my arms holding on them as my body sunk to the floor.

"I'm not ready to die. I'm not ready to die."

Rick pulled himself down to where my body sank. My hands fell and they stopped to cover my face.

"You knew you were going to be a killer, then. OK. Does that mean God wanted you to become a killer?"

"God wants me dead. I know – so I can't do anymore killing. He didn't save her. Now, he isn't saving me."

He laughed. I opened my eyes.

"You think God didn't save her?" he asked.

"He didn't. After that first time, she got beat all the way up to when she died."

"Don't you think that is when he saved her? Saved her from a lifetime of beating? Like those people I saw, she didn't want to go – to leave you – but she knew where she was going was better than staying to watch you turn into him."

I looked at him when I heard those words. Of course I turned into him.

"Is that what happened? You turned into him and... and now you think you're going to die like him? That's there no way out?"

"Two more days and God gets me dead. Going to put me in hell with the rest of 'em."

"What about all this making it right? What about those girls and your son – doesn't that count? Isn't there time to do more?"

"I can't make it right with Momma. And because I'm not sorry... because I didn't keep my promise... I can't make it right with myself."

"God doesn't want you dead. And he doesn't want you in hell."

"How do you know – how do you know that?"

"Because he's changing you. Getting you ready. He's been slowly killing you. All that's in you – all this creek rising, all this history, all this killing – is supposed to die. He's been killing you so you can live. He's been killing you so you can start over."

"How am I supposed to start over when I am about to die?"

"That's how you start over – you die. That's what your mother wanted. In that creek. She knew that's what God does in the water."

I knew, too. That's why after I shot him I pulled his body with two large stones in my hands to the deepest part of the creek. He floated a bit but I grabbed his body with my legs and laid the stones on his chest. Then I reached into the creek for more stones – bigger than the size of my hands – and rolled them on top of him.

He was staying down. He was not coming up clean. Down and up and alive again, I knew. But Daddy was staying in that creek. More and more stones pushed his body to the bottom. I backed away and couldn't see his face through the muddy water.

"Like Momma said – down and up and alive again."

"That's it, Wayne. That's it. It's exactly that. Going down in the dirty water and coming up clean."

She was clean, though, in her watery grave. That's what I saw. The water washes it all away. The water cleanses. That's what the preacher said.

I ran to the sink and cupped some water and ran it back to him, dripping most of it on the floor. I pushed my hands through the cell bars.

"Rub it on my head. Say some words. Say amen. Take it. Take it."

Rick stood there, trying to take it but the water fell to the floor. I raced down to the sink again.

"Take it. Take it. Wash it away. Clean... Clean me."

The water fell to the floor through my hands as Rick stepped back from the cell door. I ran down there again, only to stop at my bed, my hands wet.

There was no way to make me clean. There was no way to make it right with Momma. No way to make it right with anybody. No way to wash away the creek inside.

Lovell came down the row then and Rick was still a bit surprised.

"Wayne, how did this water get here?"

I sat on my bed, hands in my head, my face wet, my hands still wet. Rick answered for me.

"He was trying to, I think, to get me to baptize him."

Lovell looked inside at me.

"Wayne, you alright in there – we need to take you to see the doc?"

Wash me clean, wash me clean, wash me clean were the whispers they heard as they left me. Lovell came back with a mop and a bucket on wheels. He pushed the mop into the bucket and brought it out.

Through my eyes covering my face, I saw the dripping water fall into the bucket and the floor as he moved the mop over the floor. I closed my eyes and the black bag came. Then wetness dripped from my skull to my face. I hear Lovell reading my sentence. The volts come. I am pulled into the water and up again. Water –the creek's water – washed it all away. In heaven. My little angel.

I open my eyes and see Lovell mopping the floor.

"What you seeing Wayne?"

I am clean. I am clean. I am alive.

Chapter Eight 1904

SHE STUMBLED INTO THE water and its wetness raced up her dress. The water climbed the fabric as she lurched deeper and deeper into the water, the water that could, that would, that must clean her. She had been changed, been jarred opened, been taken – and now alone, left her with her shame.

And now she prayed what her mother said was true – the water washes it away.

She felt the surface of the water, as high as her chest. She dragged her palm over the calm waters, watching the slow current. She drew her hand down and then back up, holding the cleansing balm. She took it to the top of her other arm and let it slide down her arm. And again with the opposite hand, hoping, praying, wanting to be clean.

The water washes it away. That's what her mother told her as she was readying for marriage, only a year ago. Then, the man who would have her, who would lay with her, died, was taken by the white plague. Now, aged more than the time passed, shame was added to her sadness.

Underneath the water, as her toes pinch the sandy bottom, the water rushed through her legs. She pushed her buoyant dress back into the water, holding it between her legs. She grabbed the ruffled skirt underneath the water and began to wring it blindly.

She had bathed in this creek as a child with her brother. They were brought here in the summer to swim. And that one summer, they were brought to be cleansed, buried in the water and taken up again. Her brother had left, gone to the capital but only to return poorer. He had returned married and now lived on a part of the land that their family name had known for generations. It was magnetic, this land, this creek.

She had her way out, out of this legacy she had been given, her heritage of poverty. Away to Savannah, where he – the cotton trader – was to marry her. But now, all she had was blood on her hands.

In the water, she knew something had changed inside of her. She had come to the creek – the waters where the preacher held her and dipped her – she had come to renew that cleansing, to renew the prayers of her childhood. She rose and fell backward into the water and felt her feet rise. Floating, floating, dreaming... cleansing waters come and take me...

The entrance was guarded by a woman sucking on a snake. She was straddling the temporary steps that took those paying a dime into the circus of spectacular sights and wild sounds. Even as an adult, as a woman who could be married, Hattie held onto her father's arms. He squeezed back as he watched his last daughter, his last child walk through the curtains.

The odor of the animals clamored at their noses while the noisy crowd and bellowing announcer fought for their ears. When they entered, lights formed a ring and dimmed seats near the front. They followed the line before them and found a row unfilled. Hattie sat in the middle between her parents, who had spent everything they could in the past year to take away her emotional debt.

"Look over there, a tiger," her father said as he pointed to the ring.

She squeezed his hand again, again a little girl, again a child.

There was no hope of marriage now, a sullen and homebound girl too removed from life to be wanted. The burden on them – another mouth to feed – was felt but never shown to her. His job in Eatonton at the mill provided some, but in the months to come there would be need of more.

One of her father's acquaintances at the cotton mill joked they should take her to the circus and leave her there. Maybe she'll fall in love with an animal tamer and run away, he said. That was not their hope as they sat there, covering either side of Hattie. They only wanted her to see something happy, something fun, something that might replace her year of memories.

The tiger in the ring gnarled and clawed at the man with the whip. They circled each other, the man prodding the animal once in a while with a chair. It jumped over a grounded square box and Hattie jumped in her seat a little. Her excitement grew and she began to peer through the half-lit tent. Surely he would be there. He – the man, the strong man who commanded the animals – would be here.

Her father took her to town the day before to see the circus parade on Jefferson Street. She stood along the road watching as pairs and pairs of horses came. They pulled cages of animals and jugglers followed them on foot, throwing dishes and balls and sometimes fire into the air. Monkeys danced in the dirt street while a band provided all quarters of the small town with music.

He was the tallest man walking outside one of the cages. He held a whip and used it sparingly on a lion. His eyes were set small in his face but they caught hers. She demurred and then returned the gaze, now noticing how his shoulders held the weight of her desires.

She stood a few bodies back from his touch but he whipped the lion back from the bars and bounded up on the cage, one foot dangling above the ground. He held onto the whip and the bar with one hand and waved to the crowd, to her with the other. She heard the invitation – come one, come all.

Her father knew nothing specific of her joy but saw the smile on her face as they returned to their farm. He laid coins on her lap and her smile broadened.

"But poppa we do not have..." she said.

"Perhaps you will see something there you like," he said.

When she got home, she wandered down to the creek which ran for miles and lined the end of the family's small acres. She often went there when she wanted to be alone. It drew her, called her, whispered to her like it had so many before her.

She sat on the bank, her work dress already dirty from field work. And she exploded in bliss. She laid her back to the ground and stared at the clouds passing in unknown shapes above. She curled herself in her own arms, masking the reality of the woods with the dream of being in his hold. It had been a year – a long year – since she had felt this way, since the Lord of death came.

The jugglers rushed into the circle and the crowd cheered. They began to throw dishes and balls – three and four, and then five into the air. Then the lights shut off and a single torch was lit in the middle of the tent. Then another and another and another. Then they flew across the ring, jugglers on either side catching the flames as if by godlike hands.

She began to wonder of him. Where would he be? Yes, the lion. When would it be out? She did not know. When a skit of clowns danced into the ring pulling ladders and rolling barrels, she dug into her seat, as if disappointed.

The clowns tripped and jumped over each other for a few minutes and then she heard the crack of a whip. There she saw him, his back at first, leading a lion into the ring. He snapped the whip again forcing the animal's back to the crowd. She saw his face – that face, lit only for her. In white pants with boots and a dark black jacket, he toured the lion around the circle and snapped the whip, sitting him on his hind legs.

The crowd applauded, as did Hattie. The lion jumped over a barrel left by the clowns. He placed his front paws on the barrel and walked as the man ordered. And for a finale, the lion jumped up and licked the man's face. More applause as the pair left the ring.

"You like the lion, then?" her mother asked. Her mother was an antique replica of Hattie. All that was young in Hattie had either died or grayed in her mother. Since the death of Hattie's fiancé her mother had noticed all that was once young about Hattie – her spirit, her heart, her face – was now old. And it was in the moment of applause that she noticed those things – those things no one could touch as if to bring them to life again, things no one could give back save only the Lord – those things had returned to Hattie, as if they were personified in the lion tamer. And so the mother of the stricken one could not refuse the request.

"Can I go see the lion – Can I go outside and see it?"

Her father and mother started to get up but she pushed them down softly with her hands.

"Myself – by myself. I want to go by...myself."

And as she skirted past the rowed crowds, she turned to notice they were still looking, following her with their eyes. Outside, in the post-dusk, she saw fires burning in small rings to the left and right. She heard the applause inside, too. She made a wide path around to the other side of the tent – where she thought the animals went out – and found empty cages. She found him through two rows of cages on the steps of a train car smoking a cigar. She smiled as she walked toward him.

"A little lady I see. You come to see the animals? They'll be here – feeding time now."

He was older than her, older than her man from Savannah. He was sitting but his legs reached out far and his hands held the cigar with such temerity. But the smoke – the rings he blew – was soft and made her smile more. He arose and took the three steps between them.

"You come to see the animals... or would you like to see more?"

Hattie did not answer and when he took her hand, she did not refuse. He walked her inside the car, his firm hand driving her inward. In the darkness she could see a path that was formed between cots. They were bunks, one on top of another, dirty from the smell. The smell included all the animals then, all the circus in that squared traveling room. The emptiness of the car frightened her and in the darkness she squeezed the hand she had – forgetting it was the hand of a stranger.

"There is more back here," a voice said, now pulling her along the tight corridor.

She walked through a cloud of smoke and tripped. She stumbled and then the hand that had led her, that had comforted her in the darkness, now wrenched her into a cot. She was pushed then pulled, rammed then yanked. She was slapped then muffled, held down then tossed freely into a wall. She felt a body on top of her, smoke in its mouth, and boots kicked her shins.

She fought back with her hands – slapping the air, sometimes skin, pounding down on a massive backside – and with her legs – kicking into the air, trying, now desperate to bring her knees up. And when she could not – when she could not do what she wanted, what she must to save herself – Hattie tried to yell and that too failed.

The voice mumbled about having a girl, about long trips and perfumed dresses. The body pounded her, its hands opening her legs, its thighs like rocks she could not move. She heard jingling – a belt latch perhaps – and then he kissed her. He inserted his tongue into her mouth, forcing her to gasp for air and only receiving his air. It was met by a deeper violence, a horrible violence that pushed, pushed, pushed her eyes wide. As if she had seen evil in that darkness.

As it began, it ended. Hattie was tossed and thrown to the floor, hoisted and yanked back to standing before that body. She was twisted away from him and pushed toward the door. She was pushed into the night from the car and stumbled into the ground. Just before more applause she heard a laugh. She crawled for a few steps and rolled flat on the ground. She could not tell if her eyes were closed or open – darkness either way. The circus went on in her head.

She curled up on the thin, flat summer grass, holding her stomach with her hands. Ever so slightly her fingers crawled lower. In the darkness she could not see but she felt the stain. She was alone, alone in darkness.

And when ye spread forth your hands, I will hide mine eyes from you; yea your hands are full of blood.

She cried, wept without sound, in the silence of all that was lost. She wept in the darkness that came from heaven.

She found herself on her knees, bent over, still holding her stomach with one hand, the other keeping her off the ground. She looked forward and saw the circus tent alive with light. She looked left and then right and saw shadows near fires. She brought herself to her feet and stumbled toward a fire.

When she got close enough to scare them off, they ran – black figures, clothed in rags. She was alone again. The heat from the fire pushed her away again into the darkness. No one could help her, no one could make her clean.

There was no car this evening. They had walked, taken a path along the creek from the house to a massive clearing where the circus had planted its stakes. And so, then, Hattie began to stagger toward the water.

They found her crawling out of the water. When they did not find her near the lions or the tigers or any of the cages, they thought she had headed home. Her father got there first, holding her from falling one more time. As her mother arrived, she saw what the creek could not take away. It was her shriek that forced her husband to push Hattie back from his chest, revealing the violence done to her.

Her mother screamed.

Her father shook her and the words that were in her mouth were thrust back into her trance-bound mind. She closed her eyes and he shook her again, thinking her dead. He picked her up and laid her next to the bank. Her mother was on her knees next to him patting Hattie's hair. Her father splashed water on her face and she looked at him.

"Tell me. Tell me. What happened? Who did this?" he said.

The first memory was the fires she saw – crawling toward the fire and seeing the black figures scatter. The heat she felt on her face, reddening the skin, already filled with indignity. She did not see the car and the darkened passage. Though the violation was real, was true, it was also harsh and indescribable, erased, enveloped in blackness.

All she could see, all she could feel, all she could say was darkness. There was darkness, poppa, darkness all around, black darkness.

They took her back to the house and laid her in a bed. Hattie heard nothing else except her father on the phone.

"My girl's been raped. By a colored – she said a group of them – all dark – raped her at the circus."

Hattie felt her mother put a wet cloth on her head. Then she saw her father standing in the doorway, lit by a candle, holding a gun.

It took a few minutes to run back along the creek, back along the waters his father had run through, his grandfather had killed in. He came to the circus field and saw the fires still burning.

By then the sheriff was there and they roamed the grounds. A group of blacks stood near a fire. They were the only blacks working for the circus. It had not brought its kitchen workers to Georgia because they did not want to come. But four cotton workers were paid to clean the cages during the show.

"This is them. They did it – she said it was them," her father said.

"There ain't no more like you working here?" the sheriff asked.

They shook their heads. More neighbors had arrived carrying guns. Hattie's father filled them in with loud words while the sheriff tied the group together with chains and led them from the fire. By the time the sheriff had walked the gang to the city jail nearly the whole town was there – mostly men, mostly with guns, some with torches, some only with rage in their hands.

The jail was a rock fortress with battlements on top and an oak door that when the sheriff swung it open looked a foot thick to the prisoners. Fear gave some room to safety. But there they stood, faces lit by the torches held by the hands of death, still in front of the mob. They looked out into the crowd and knew there was no going inside. There was no safety inside the castle and no safety outside.

The sheriff unshackled them one by one. After each felt freedom, the crowd reminded them by promise they were not. We gonna kill you. We gonna hang you for what you done. When they were unchained, they stood motionless. No one left. Except the sheriff.

Hattie's father walked up to the first free man. He knew what was inside of him. He knew he had slain the Indians. He knew what the others – cousins, nephews, uncles and grandmothers – knew: that in the generations since the creek had invaded his name. He knew he could. He was ready, ready to kill.

"You the one who took my little girl to the circus?"

"No, sir. We be standing..."

He fired a shot into the left foot and asked the now crouching man the same question.

"We know you the one who raped my girl. Say it."

"No..."

A shot into the right foot. The man could no longer stand so Hattie's father moved to the next one.

"What about you? You the one who raped my Hattie?"

The criminal said nothing.

"Speak up boy. Say it."

The criminal refused to confess, shaking his head in both fear and denial. He bowed his head and closed his eyes to receive his punishment but none came. Hattie's father had moved to the next one. Same response twice more.

Hattie's father stepped back into a line of men with guns. Each raised their aim.

"We gonna ask again. And we gonna get you to say it."

The criminals answered all at once, gibberish that confessed nothing except fear. Each received a wound in the leg and all fell to ground.

Hattie's father handed his gun to another and went back to the first in line, now curled up at his feet, lying in his own blood.

"You the one who did it?"

A grunt that he took as denial, a moan he took as defiance came. He took out a knife and sliced the animal's left arm at the wrist. He sliced three more wrists after the others refused to answer.

"This gonna be your last chance. Tell us what we wanna hear."

The silence confirmed their guilt and the jury handed up their sentence. Guns fired on and on, muffled through the city, shouting justice in the hollow, echoing through the past.

When he came home that night, Hattie's father went into her room. She turned over from his pull and saw his sleepless eyes look into her.

"They got what was coming to 'em," he said.

Her mother came over as he left and smoothed the cloth on her head.

Through the night, the evil she saw in the darkness woke her, suffocating her, and she awoke needing breath to find her way back to reality. She felt it all again that first night.

In the morning a doctor came. He told her to dream as he opened her. She closed her eyes and tried to think of her childhood, when the creek was cool on a summer's day, when she splashed her brother. But she felt the grass on her palms and she stumbled through her mind.

The doctor assured her she was healing well. He left and her mother sat beside her, smoothing the cloth on her head.

"I think I remember more about it. There was a..."

"Don't try. Rest."

"There was a train. But I am not sure. It leaves me and comes back."

Her mother listened but did not speak.

"What did Poppa do last night?"

"He took care of them. Them who did this to you."

Hattie could only remember one body. She could see only one pair of hands on her. But perhaps she was confused.

"How many were there?" she asked.

"There were four, cleaning the cages."

"And what did Poppa do?"

"He and the sheriff took them to the jail."

"Did Poppa...?"

And her mind raced to the newspaper she read a few years ago. Those men – those men who raped that woman – were burned and then hanged. Her mother knew, too, and reluctantly answered.

"Those dogs," her mother said, looking down at her hands. "He did what needed to be done."

Over the next week, Hattie's nightmares slowed and as they did they became foggier. The darkness had receded but it took with it the identity of the rapist. She was not sure of anything except what had her poppa had done. She was convinced because of the justice he did. But she only remembered what she was convinced of: that it was bound to be true that one of them did rape her.

Hattie prayed and prayed and hands were laid on her, even the preacher came and petitioned God to not allow the horrible wickedness to continue. But as the weeks turned into a month, it was clear she was carrying a child. So she had stopped doing any work for her mother and spent her mornings in bed. She did not go into town anymore, a stigma in her soul, in her belly.

A new nightmare started during the fall. The darkness she saw came back, in the form of a face, a dark face with four sets of eyes. But these new nightmares were not of the past but the future. The face spoke whispers about drops of blood invading her family, lines of life being tainted. They taunted her with pictures of mulatto generations. And they laughed when she tried to deny it, tried to clean her bloody hands. Rape was the first shame; the child became the second.

She ran one morning in tears to her mother, haunted by the faces. Her mother rushed to her and held her, wrapping her hands around her head. She walked Hattie to a chair and squatted in front of her.

"Why aren't you still sleeping?"

"I can't. When I close my eyes, they tease me."

"Who? Who teasing you?"

"Them – the monsters. They..." Hattie said as she put her hands over her face. She quickly removed them. "They're there – laughing."

"What are they saying?"

"That they did it to make us dirty, give us them – give us their blood. Forever."

Her mother grabbed her head again.

"Oh, my baby. Blood ain't gonna ruin us. Blood ain't gonna ruin this family."

But as Hattie felt her mother's grip on her head, she knew that same grip was hopeless on the promise she made. The Lord had cursed this family, blood and all. She was the carrier, but she would not be damned, would not damn this family. Her child was the cursed one.

The months grew into winter and the holidays flew through. It seemed the town had forgotten what Hattie's father had done, though Hattie had not. She sat with her father next to the fire after the new year passed and told him about the dream she had the night before.

"I saw you shooting them. I saw you doing what you did. But it was like you were doing it somewhere I didn't know. There was no jail, nobody else, just you and them four. And you told them all about me and how they had taken me from you."

He stoked the fire, poking deep into an ashen log.

"They got what was coming to 'em. Doing what they did – and having this child."

In the fire in front of her, she saw the fire that night. She felt its warmth and crossed her hands on her shoulders. Then she saw her father running through the grass, gun in hand, aiming to that fire. The growing flames jolted her back to reality.

"Poppa, tell me what you did that night."

"We found you at the creek – all wet and crying. I ran down the creek and met the sheriff. He took them back to the jail."

"Did you ask the sheriff to go? Did he knew what you were gonna do?"

"He knew, Hattie. He knows about me, about this creek, about where I come from... He knew what I was gonna do."

"How come they never confessed?"

"I guess they wanted to die quick."

"Did you watch them die? What did they see?"

He thought about that question for a moment. He saw himself whisper into their ears. He saw his bullets fly, only his bullets, enter that darkness.

"They suffered, like they should."

"Did the sheriff even talk to you about it?"

"He knew what had to be done – them boys were not gonna last long even if he was there. He couldn't protect them."

"Do you think you would do it again?"

"Defend my family?"

"No, Poppa. Just shoot someone. Kill 'em."

"I'd kill 'em if they..."

He paused and looked at her. He saw what he did not want to see. He saw what had to be true, but denied for so long: it was in her, too.

He poked at a large log in the fire, breaking it in half. Hot coals settled to the bottom and smoke scurried up the chimney and over the creek, the creek that was the blood of this line.

She woke up in a sweat, her bed wet. She knew it was time. She screamed for them and they came. They drew her up against the wall and called the doctor. By the time he arrived, she was pushing.

The pain doubled inside of her as the darkness came again. Each agony in the cold morning house produced in the nightmare an agony: her head hitting the wall, her face being slapped, or her body being thrown against the cot. She squeezed her eyes shut with each push and heard herself scream. She watched herself, felt herself being taken, the memory longer than the night.

The first announcement came: I see its head, the doctor said, his face lit by a lamp to the side. And then after she pushed and pushed and tried to push him off, tried desperately to push him off, it was over. The rush of the finish took her to the creek, the current running through her legs.

It was there she saw what had to be done.

The doctor left after checking Hattie one last time. Her mother put the baby in a blanket after washing it. Her father came to her bedside and squeezed her hand. He looked at her and saw what he had hoped would go away, what his father and fathers before had promised would come. He saw his eyes staring back at him, eyes wet with the evil waters he had inside.

Poppa, take me to the creek.

He knew it had come to her. And he knew, too, that it would be a good killing. He patted his only daughter on her head and promised he would take her, as soon as she could walk. She closed her eyes, seeing the darkness, feeling her father's hand.

When she rose, he led her to the waters, the waters that would clean the blood. They took the baby wrapped in swaddling clothes and laid him in the water, the cold water that would keep flowing in them, they knew. But in this time, to this land, there was a heritage worse than the creek.

They kept their hands on its head, father and daughter, hands of the same, the creek rising up and up and up on them. And they buried the wickedness in the creek. Their shared prayer was silent but ineffective: If it had not been the Lord who was on our side, then the raging waters would have gone over our souls.

Chapter Nine 1954

HE TOLD THEM NO HOTEL the night before, no going through town – no sign at all there were federal agents anywhere. They had to come that morning – damn the hours from Atlanta, it's my life you're taking – and take the wide line around Eatonton. No FBI hats, no FBI suits, no FBI cars – nothing that a driver heading the other way would notice. Those were his orders, the best line of defense Leonard Mathis could think of.

He sped along the highway, his hands gripping the wheel. He adjusted the mirror again and again to look behind him but the dust storm was the only follower. That made him nervous. He was certain no one knew – especially his brother Lester – really knew where he was going. There was some safety in that thought. Then again those who didn't know – especially his wife – were the weak link.

In the middle of the day after he declined to share a sandwich with his brother at the garage they ran in town, Leonard took his Pontiac south along the route to Macon. He told his brother he was going home to check on his pregnant wife and eat there. He would be back in an hour. In that hour she could call the garage and then Lester might be looking for him, too.

As his car bumped onto the bridge near their land, the waters of Murder Creek, the creek that was their blood, flowed on and on. It's ain't gonna get me, too, he thought to himself. That creek's ain't gonna swallow me.

A man dressed in overalls was waiting underneath the old fire tower off Rabbit Run Road, looking over a map. Leonard had chosen a place very few people knew about – one being Lester, he conceded to himself – and one that was hard to find. Rabbit Run was not on any map – the only sign of its existence was the large oak tree that had become the landmark for the corner. The long dirt road ended at the fire tower.

Leonard pulled into the clearing underneath the tower and shoved the car into park. He turned it off and looked at the man standing near the open bed of a red truck that had no plates and squares of pine straw in the back. He laughed, though the sadness he had come with stopped it short.

He had his family, his land, and he had his brother. They were brothers, twins, born to a poor family who had no place but this. It was hard to tell them

92

apart. They smoked, they married and had one son, and they shared the only garage in town. They shared their father's penance for fishing. And they lived near Murder Creek as their family had lived for years, listening to the same stories on their grandfather's knee. Leonard had turned informer, an attempt to stop, to dam the creek inside.

In that moment when his smile was shattered by sadness, in his memory he heard the echoes of the gunshot –the single shot that exploded his father's brain. Here was a place very few people knew about, the place his father added one more to the line, the long line, the line that flowed like the creek that cursed his name. The line of killers from Murder Creek, their victims floating like ghosts over the water, buried in the water, like his momma said.

The man folded the map and threw it into an open window and took steps toward the Pontiac. Leonard opened his door and stepped in front of the car. From the pockets of the overalls a badge flipped open.

"I know who you are," he said.

"Just protocol, Leonard," the man said. "I'm George Merton."

"You the one the FBI sent?"

"Like you said – got that truck from some guy south of Atlanta. And these" he said plucking the strap on the overalls, "that guy gave them to me – said I looked like I was some federal agent or something."

They stood there in the summer silence long enough for Leonard to doubt one more time. This wasn't about rights and politics. Snitching – if that's what anybody wanted to call it – was something he did for something more personal. He wasn't scared of dying for what he was doing. He was scared of living – living with what he heard over and over on his grandfather's knee.

It ain't gonna get me. It ain't in me no more.

He looked around at the woods and ran his eyes up the tower. He pointed at the covered area at the summit of the stairs.

"My father shot himself from the top of that tower. When I was 14. Almost 20 years now. Lester don't remember it as well as I do. I found the body."

Drunk and missing for three days, the twins traced up and down the creek in the middle of winter. Then each took a neighbor's hound and took off in different directions on the highway. It was not until Leonard got to that tree – some two miles away from the house – that the dog found something. It led him down the dirt road to the tower.

Then the wire fence around the clearing was sturdy. One had to crawl underneath it – something only a child could do – or climb a small tree in one corner and jump over the top of the fence. Leonard crawled up the tree, the same tree he knew his father had, and jumped into the belly of the tower. In the middle a stairway led to the top.

He raced as fast as he could to the top. When he stepped up onto the last level, he noticed the dirty windows and closed door. He peered into one window to see his father's palm open, the gun lying on it. His father had locked the door so Leonard kicked it in and hurried to his knees at his father's side. The bullet had destroyed part of his face, but he was still alive.

Leonard took off his shirt and tried to wrap his father's cheek but his hand was startled by another and then a moan by his father.

"Finish it," the half-dead voice whispered, emanating from the corner of his mouth. "Finish me."

His father tried to grip his palm over the gun and it was then Leonard's mind processed his father's last words. Leonard tried to tilt his father's head once last time so he could speak, but the groan answered.

He tried to leave us. I hate him. I'll do it.

He tried to, but he's still alive. I can't do it.

What if he lives? What if everyone knows? What if he lives? I'll do it.

What are you saying, Daddy? I understand. I understand. I'll finish it.

Leonard reached for the gun, checked it for one more bullet, and fired into his father's head– sending an echo through the woods to his brother's ears and through the eras of time. He stood there as the temporal gave way to eternal and watched his father lose his fight with the creek. A fight that now had taken to him.

Lester turned his dog around and ran down the highway toward the sound. He turned at the corner tree and stopped at the secured area as his brother slowly crawled down the tree trunk outside the fence.

"What was that shot? Is he up there?"

Leonard kept the truth from his brother, hoping the creek would only take one of them.

"He's dead, Lester. I didn't get to him before... He's dead. Up there."

Their mother – herself to become a drunk – said it was his way, their way. She forced the twins to drag the body down from the tower and bury him in the church's cemetery across the highway after a preacher refused to honor the hell he said their father was in.

"He's buried just down the road here. My mother – before she drank herself to death years later – used to go on and on about this place, this creek... ghosts and killers... and...adding another to the line."

The FBI man brought his gaze from the tower but sought solace in the trees. Lester's eyes were too demanding.

The meeting fought its way through the honking and the whiskey inside Leonard's head that night as he grabbed the wheel with both hands. He rolled up the window, silencing the column of cars behind him and closing off the nighttime summer stick.

He drank another swig from the bottle beside him. The alcohol hid the fear created by that conversation beneath the tower. He prayed it smothered the creek – or did it unleash it?

From the backseat of the car in front, Lester's son Michael could see the dust along the windows, high and swift. He saw the beams of headlights paint his father's body in the driver's seat. He eyed his father's hand empting another bottle into his mouth and tossing it out the window. Michael could hear the horns and engines of the cars behind him. Then the tires bumped onto a bridge and even in the dark midnight to 11-year-old Michael that signaled only one thing: they were near home.

Lester rolled up his window after hearing the bottle crack against the outside. He honked the horn and grabbed the wheel with both hands and slung the car right, throwing his son against the door. After righting himself the boy looked out the opposite window and saw his house lit by a lone, tall, orange light atop a pole. They were not headed home just yet. They were headed to the creek.

After the turn Lester made another sharp turn of the wheel right, sending the car down into a clearing that sat off the bridge. Back to the left again and the car stopped. Michael inched his eyes above the door to see the dark creek outside. Three others cars pulled into the clearing, leaving their headlights on.

"Poppa, what we stopping here for?"

"Boy, don't ask no more questions. Just stay in the car."

Lester opened and slammed his door and took a second bottle with him to the trunk. Along the way he threw the top into the night. Michael watched men from the other cars walk past his window, their faces in and out of the headlights. Michael raced his head to the back, following them to the trunk.

"We gonna make him run scared, Leonard," he said to his brother. "Hold this while I get the key."

"Why you bring the kid, Lester?" Leonard asked.

"It's his introduction," he said with a smile. "His momma was tired of him."

Lester fumbled with the keys, dropping them to the ground. He kicked with his shoe and struck the keys. He bent over and rattled them in his hand.

"Now we gonna see how he runs," he said before taking a swig from the bottle.

The trunk light exposed a dark figure, his hands reaching up to cover his fading pupils. The light revealed sweat on his legs and shirtless torso. Lester, Leonard, and the others grab legs and arms and hurl the young black boy out of the trunk. Someone slams it shut, giving Michael his view.

The kidnapped stays on all fours. Someone grabs his head from behind. Another shines a light in his face, revealing the blood and busted skin. Lester bends down to the colored face.

"You don't put up much of a fight, do you boy? You scared?" he said, slapping the right cheek.

Lester barked for the handler to straighten the target and then a boot came from the left to send him to his knees. Someone else kicked him in the side, sending him to the dirt.

"Boy, we don't like our colored dirty," Lester said. "But this here creek gonna clean you right up."

Lester kicks at the boy, forcing him to roll into the creek. The splash sends jubilation through the crowd. Lester takes another swig and pushes the boy's face into the water. The bottle breaks over the black hair. Then Lester wades into the water a bit and drags the boy erect. He pulls out a pistol from his belt and points it at the boy's temple.

"How 'bout it, boys?"

They raise their hands and voices. One shoots off a round into the air.

"Now this here boy wants to go to school with our daughters. This here boy wants to play on our football team. Ain't that right, boy?"

Michael noticed the slow trickle of blood coming from the boy's lips and the dirt like patches on his sweaty legs and stomach. He saw his father cock the gun.

"Well, there ain't gonna be no school, no team. Because you know what that sound is, boy? That's the last sound you gonna hear."

The gun fires, the hammer hitting an empty chamber. The target lurches back in surprise and stumbles into the creek even more.

"That's right – run, boy," Lester yells.

The boy – dazed by the life he still has and the order his body can't comply with at the moment – rights himself a little and looks at Lester.

"I said run, boy," he said as he cocked and fired again, the flash of powder sending a bullet flying past the target. The boy takes off down the creek, running from shots from the bank and from Lester.

Michael sees his father take out a rag from his pocket and pour some alcohol over it. He sticks the rag into the bottle and ignites it with a metal lighter. He tosses it up the creek and it explodes near the boy, sending him into the water. The dark night sky is lit with a runaway and the eruption of laughter through the bodies of the men on the bank.

"Go on, boy. Keep running. You ain't fast enough for our team," Lester says.

The crowd returns to their cars and Michael watches as his father stands in front of his car smoking. Leonard walks up and takes a puff from his brother's cigarette. He had to congratulate his brother, as he had always done.

"You got him good with the bottle," Leonard said.

"Hell, I might kill the next one. Then we just float him down this creek like all the rest," his arm leading the way down the water for his words.

Lester smiled and tossed the lit stick to the ground. Leonard turned to leave but Lester grabbed him by the arm and whispered into his ear.

"Kill 'em just like we're supposed to."

Lester left and slammed the door on his own car after getting in.

"Your granddaddy would be proud, son," he says as he turns on the car. "Me and Leonard doing him right."

The car revs up to the road and across it. The bumpy dirt driveway ends at the lone light. Michael darts out to the front porch and waits for his staggering father.

They terrorized that summer. They met at Lester's house every night and rumbled through town after dark, headlights off around the courthouse square. They caught one walking alone at night and snatched two from the dusk in the city proper. Each time the eyes revealed the fear of that chamber they did not know was empty. Leonard watched and shot stray bullets into the night like the rest, hoping Lester would not find one who would offer resistance. That hope, though, was already being drowned by their grandfather's stories flooding reality.

Word came to Lester that week some colored boys had begun to swim upstream in Murder Creek. In the garage and at the house that night Lester raged about black blood and black sweat and all blackness filtering from upstream.

They waited until dark when the swimmers slowly emerged from the woods onto a dirt road. Black bodies scattered in five directions as Lester flipped on his headlights. His Pontiac led the chase of one thin-boned boy down the road, leaving the other swimmers safe. The dirt road led nowhere and finally the exhausted prey tumbled to the ground trying to climb the steep embankment.

Leonard exited slowly from his shotgun seat in the Pontiac and watched others run past him to help his brother tackle the squirming victim. They brought him to his feet and pulled his arms behind and tied them with rope. They stood him up in the light like the showcasing of a hunted deer. Leonard leaned against the front bumper as his brother's body blocked the path of the boy in front of his car. The light broke on both sides of Lester's body, darkening his face as he began taunting.

"Boy, who said you and your friends could swim in my creek?"

No answer. Lester used his right pointer to bring the boy's gaze up from the ground.

"I asked you a question, boy. Who said you could put your black body in my water?"

"We ain't know sir..."

Leonard twisted the boy's finger to silence him.

"My family been living on this creek since..." and he turned to Leonard. "This here my brother, Leonard. Leonard how long we been living on this creek?"

Leonard did not hesitate.

"Since the 1700s.'"

"And how long do you suppose we've been washing our clothes in it and getting baptized in it?"

"About just as long."

"So Leonard, what do you think we should do then when our creek has become – what's the word? the word they use now? – integrated?"

There was a pause but Lester answered his own question.

"I think we ought to show him our creek."

The others roared behind the scared swimmer and one of the two holding him threw him to the ground in front of Lester. The boy kicked his feet as if to free himself and his arms wriggled but to no avail.

"Look at him boys. He's trying to swim. He's trying to swim like a fish. I've caught a fish in my creek."

They bound his ankles with more rope and stuffed him in the trunk of Lester's Pontiac and drove through town. Inside the lead car, Lester chatted as if they were working in the garage. The revolver sat between them. Lester picked up the gun while handling the steering with the other hand.

"There is some bullets in the dash – load it. But leave the first empty."

Leonard opened the dash and collected the bullets. As he filled the slots he recognized the history in his hand.

"I didn't know you kept this – from Daddy. All these years?"

He handed the gun over to his brother and Lester took a firing grip on it. He pointed toward his window.

"Yep. That bastard shot himself with it and now I'm using it. Some people say you use a dead man's gun it's cursed. It ain't cursed."

Perhaps he had taken it when they dragged the body down. Or afterward. Perhaps then he knew there were two bullets missing from the loaded cylinder. Leonard flipped on the radio: Wanted. Someone I trusted, who gave no warning.

"Hell, you gonna hit one of them someday," Leonard said as he turned off the music. "Firing off into the night like you do when they run."

Lester set the gun back on the seat between them and rubbed his hand into the steering wheel.

"It ain't the gun that cursed, Leonard. We are. The bastard added one more to the line."

A honk came from the caravan and the car bumped over the bridge and Lester swerved it down into the clearing. The others followed, encircling the Pontiac with the fish inside. As Leonard pulled out of the car, Lester reached over to the dash and fingered one more bullet.

They dragged the boy from the trunk, untied him, and stood him near the water facing the row of headlights. The brothers leaned back on the closed trunk to watch the others whack the backside of the boy with a leather strap. When he fell over, they kicked him. When he tried to talk they slapped his face.

The ritual continued as Lester walked up to the bloodied but erect boy.

"You got your own pools, your own water, your own schools. And you want my creek. Isn't that right, boy?"

"No sir..." Leonard silenced him with the gun to his chin. He pulled away and took a step to the side. He planted the gun on the boy's temple and cocked it.

"I believe this boy here wants to swim. Should we let him swim?"

A chorus of yes came and Lester walked the boy into the water up to his shins. Lester pushed the boy hard enough to force him on all fours.

"Come on, now, boy. Show us how you swim."

The boy squirmed and kicked at the water and then Lester tugged on his hair. He pulled him from the water and made him stand again. He pointed the gun again at the side of his skull and cocked it.

"You know what that sound is, boy? That's the last sound you gonna hear."

In that instant, the killers and their victims of the creek cried in agony from the waters. The bullet blasted the black skin and tore through the skull. Lester felt the strange sensation of time wrapping itself around him, showing him not just every angle of his first killing, but every moment of killing in the stories he had now become. For Leonard, time raced on and he saw the generations to come, the killers and victims to come, appearing as premonitions on the water's surface.

The black body fell to the ground and produced one long, terrible thud.

Smoke slowly dissipated over the surface of the creek. Leonard and the others looked on, half in fear, half in shock. A glass bottle broke after being dropped from one hand. Another man took a long gulp from his bottle. One found the power to speak.

"Lester, we always... Don't you have an empty... Lester, you killed him."

"It was bound to happen sometime. I guess I loaded it wrong."

Lester spun the cylinder with his finger and kicked the body. Leonard walked up to the body and knelt to feel its arms. Both felt the death at their feet.

"What we gonna do now Lester?" one of the others asked.

"None of those swimmers got a good look at us. And we killed the one who did. Let's drag him into the creek and put some rocks on top of him."

"Shouldn't we at least leave him somewhere where they'll bury him good?"

"This creek will bury him good. And with no body we ain't got no worries. Just keep your mouth shut like we been doing and nobody will know nothing."

Lester stepped across the body to stand with his brother and barked out orders to the other men. They gathered around the body as pallbearers and walked it hip-deep into the water. Two men held the corpse while the others laid heavy stones on top of it.

"Get it good, now. Don't want it floating downstream," Lester said as the stones sank the body.

When they finished the interment, the others shook Lester's hand or patted him on the shoulder and left in the caravan. Leonard remained squatted at the spot of the thud. Darkness hid the ground, but he smoothed the sand with his hand, stopping short of the blood stain nearby.

"I kept one round out."

Lester stood facing the creek, watching the spot where the body lay, the moonlight giving just enough to the surface of the water.

"Yeah, you did."

"So it was full?"

"It was. I grabbed one more out of the dash as you were getting out."

Leonard stood up and walked to his brother. He grabbed him by the shoulder, twisting Lester's face to his own.

"You made them all killers, you know that," he said, pointing to the water.

Lester pushed his brother back in the darkness.

"Who's gonna tell? Who they gonna tell? The boys didn't know what was gonna happen."

"You did."

"And you didn't? Like we're supposed to. Isn't that what he said? Hell, I remember. 14. That old man told us then – we were gonna be like him," Lester said as he tossed a small rock into the flowing waters.

"And you decided tonight was a good time to start?"

"It was bound to happen..."

"It's got to stop with us, Lester. It's got to stop somewhere. All them stories, all of what the creek is..."

"It's already started. For me."

Leonard knew then his father had failed. Still he spoke with hope.

"Daddy tried to stop it. He tried to end..."

"He shot himself cause he was broke and didn't want us to know it."

The silence between the brothers was a wall, blocking the truth inside Leonard reaching his brother. Lester raised his gun and peered as if he were targeting a bird on a tree across the creek.

"Add one more to the line. There ain't no stopping it, no changing it," he said. "It's Murder Cre..."

Leonard grabbed the gun from his brother and spun Lester to him. He held him by the collar with one hand. The other brandished the butt of the gun.

"So how many more? How many more with this? How many of them? How many more of us? How many more gonna be cursed? It ain't gonna swallow my boy or no one else."

Lester pushed his brother away.

"It's in them, Leonard," he said, pointing over his brother's shoulder in the direction of their houses. "Whether you like it or not. It's in you like it's in me. How you gonna stop it?"

Leonard turned the gun around and pointed the gun at his brother.

"With this."

"You just gonna shot me – your own brother, your own blood? What's that gonna do? That'll just make you a killer. You don't want to believe it, Leonard, but you're like me. It's rising in you right..."

"You ain't the first for me."

"Who then? Who did you kill?"

"I shot Daddy."

Lester stared at his brother through the gun's barrel. He took a step toward him and tried to reach out for the gun. Leonard stepped back.

"I shot him. He was alive when I got there, still alive from the first shot. He asked me to finish it. So I did. He was my first."

"And I'm gonna be your second? Who would have thought? Stories about lynchings and drownings. And now it's us. Like Cain and Abel, huh? You know that story, Leonard? So when you shoot me, what does that make you?

"The one who is alive."

"The one who is cursed. You kill me and you're gonna be living with it for a long..."

"I've been living with it long enough."

"Is that what you said to the FBI man?"

Leonard's hand wavered a bit at the truth.

"That's what you been doing, ain't it? Turning on your brother. I know you don't care about the coloreds. It was always about me – about Murder Creek – about how you had to kill Daddy and how you thought you could stop all this, stop the creek. Before I thought, hell, I kill you and they would come – all the white shirts and black suits they can find. Hunt me down like a fugitive, make me hide in the woods, sleep under the bridge, run this creek. But pointing that at me, you did me a favor. I kill you now, it's defending myself. I guess you better shoot me then, Leonard. If you can. Then tell the FBI you did..."

A car bumped over the bridge and the headlights jumped into the air. Leonard turned his head a bit to see and Lester took his chance. He tackled his brother at the waist, sending him into the blood stain on the ground. Leonard flipped his brother over toward the water and Lester returned the move and both rolled into the water.

They exchanged punches with wet hands. Lester pushed his brother's face into the water with both hands. He felt a knee between his legs and took the pressure off. Leonard flipped on top, sending the pair further into the creek. The current was soft still at that point and both ended up on their hands and knees. They searched in the dark with strained eyes for the gun but neither saw it.

Lester clawed a handful of wet sand from the bottom and threw into his brother's eyes. The distraction gave him time to rise to his feet and punch Leonard in the face and then kick him in the stomach. Keeled over, the creek rushing past him, Leonard tried to grab his brother's ankles but water ran through his fingers. Another kick to the stomach and one to the head broke him.

Lester turned his brother on his stomach in the shallow water. He forced his head to stay under by rubbing his face into the mud. He kicked him over and then stomped on his stomach. Leonard groaned as his brother pulled him downstream a bit. He stomped over him again and grabbed Leonard's hair to yank his face up. He leaned over and whispered.

"I wanted you to see me. I wanted you to see it in me. Add one more to the line."

After one more thrust, this time against a rock, Lester stood back from the corpse and watched the creek flood over it, swallowing it whole. The waters flowed on and on.

Chapter Ten

THE LIGHT, THE SUN, is so bright. I squint and blink and try to pull my hand up. The chains go taut and I know I am not dreaming.

Everything's changed. Everything's gone. My house – Momma's house – gone. There is nothing there – no foundation, nothing. Nothing that says I was there, that Momma was ever there. I am home and it is gone. This is Momma's parade to nowhere.

After the van bumps onto the bridge over Murder Creek, I know the boat ramp is coming. Yes, the rocky turn-off. Everything that happened flashes. Each second more to see, more to forget, all fast becoming nothing, not even memories. A radio crackles.

"There," Lovell says to the receiver, pointing to a sign with a large red arrow showing the way to a chicken processing plant. "The road should be just past that sign."

The sheriff's deputy leading us pulls over and we turn right after the cruiser onto a dirt road that is another change to me. It's all new. The road is smooth, like after the county comes and flattens it. The ridges are high and the woods to the right block my view of the boat ramp clearing. To the left more empty land, with a wire fence around it. In the distance the chicken plant.

"Should be up here on left, Wayne," Lovell says. "As far as I know."

Momma's church should be there – it should – but everything is green. Trees covered in vines and tall, thin grass mark a corner of the intersection of the dirt road we are on and one to the left. The reporter didn't say anything about it being gone. Maybe he thought I knew.

The vans stops just before the turn. Lovell turns around to me and talks through the cage that separates us.

"Wayne, this is where it's at. It don't look like much – hell we don't even know what's in all that – but as far as I know your momma is buried there. That's where they say the cemetery is. We gonna have to shackle you – you know that – and Wayne... don't do anything without asking. You hear?"

I nod and try to scoot toward the door, but the chains keep me.

"We'll get that. Give it a second," Lovell says.

The guard in front of me slides open the door and gets out. The one behind me follows him and they point their guns at me. Lovell steps into the row with me and unlocks me from the seat. He takes my hand and helps me to the door. I set my feet on the rail and he pulls me out.

In the middle of nowhere now, nowhere near anything I knew, freedom isn't what I thought it would be. I know the creek is somewhere beyond the woods and the cemetery sits behind me. But of all the times I imagined coming back, I never saw it like this.

The sun to my right blinds me again. To my left the dirt road goes on down a hill.

"What's down that way?" I ask, the one who should know.

"The map said this is Murder Creek Church Road. Must go somewhere."

The driver has his own gun now, too. He and the other two walk backward toward the front of the van, still watching me with their barrels. Lovell walks with me.

"They going to do that all day?" I ask.

"Just have to Wayne."

I turn the front corner of the van and see the ridges of the road go up to my knees.

"How am I going to get up there with these?"

"Maybe there's a way in around the other road that isn't so high. Let's try there," Lovell says.

We walk up the road a bit and see the same ridges. But the thick woods end and we stand there looking at the chicken plant in the distance through the grass.

"I guess this is better than back there," Lovell says. "All right. You three get on up there."

The guards turn their guns away and step back from us. They run and jump the ridge and land on their feet, one after another, using their gun as balance.

"All right now, one of you keep on the gun. The others help pull Wayne up."

I walk up to the ridge and give each guard one of my hands. They pull me up while my feet try to find holds along the ridge. My shoes slip and one hits something hard and my left shoe flicks off. Lovell laughs and tosses it to the guard aiming the gun. After I'm up and hopping on one foot, he bends down and forms it on my foot. Then Lovell takes the jump and we're all in the grassy area.

The guards back their way around the heavy, thick woods and they look at Lovell. I look through the trees to find anything. Getting through all that with these chains is going to hurt. I won't be able to move under or to the side or push stuff out of the way.

"I guess we just walk as far as we can," Lovell says.

The guards turn from me and walk into the weeds and we follow. They use their guns to brush away the limbs blocking the path. The guards stop and part so Lovell and I see what they see.

When we came up in the van there was nothing but weeds and grass and trees and thorns and nowhere to go. Now, just beyond a small iron fence was the historical marker, and beyond that, the cemetery, just as I had hoped. And the fence's section right ahead was missing, left open for us.

To the right, just outside the fence, in the heavy brush was a large pile of bricks.

"I guess that's all that is left of the building," Lovell said, noticing the pile. "How long you say your family been at this church?"

"Someone in my family killed the first preacher."

"Your momma tell you that?" Lovell asks.

I nod.

"Maybe he's buried right here," one of the guards says with a laugh.

The driver steps into the fenced-off area and squats down to read a tombstone.

"When was the last time someone was buried here? It looks like this place hasn't been used for a long..." and his voice trails off as he tries to read the year on the stone. "I can't make it out. Anybody famous here?"

"My momma."

He laughs and stands erect again and points his gun at me.

"All right, Wayne, you know where to go. Show us."

I walk up to the marker and try to touch the rusted letters with my fingers. The chains stop me. I see the strange letters.

"I used to read this. Momma used to make me read this."

Yes, Momma, the waters of life. That's what the Creeks called it.

I step right and see an outline of bricks, just two high, in front of a stone. But it wasn't broken. I move past it. Don't be playing in that cemetery. No, Momma, I won't step on any graves. I pick up my feet as much as I can to the next one. It is a pointed column made of stone. I raise my chained hands and set them on top.

"Is that it?" Lovell asks.

Catch your breath – won't be no more running if you don't got your breath. They coming – coming to get you. Give me one last look at you. No, Momma, I can't. I've done something. Something bad.

"147," I whisper to myself. But who knows how far it goes, Momma.

"Wayne – is that it?" he asks again, with a sterner tone.

There are two names that have stuck with me my whole life. The name of the creek in Indian and the name of the man whose stone I put Momma under.

"Walter Hollister."

"What?" Lovell asks.

"Walter Hollister. 1865 to 1910."

"Who's that?"

"That's what it should say on the stone. Where Momma is. I don't remember where exactly."

"You mean your momma is buried in another person's grave?"

"I took a broken stone – it's got a hand on it holding a piece of chain, and one finger is pointing to the chain – I took that and put in front of her."

Lovell points the guards to look for the stone. I make an effort as well, though my shackles give me little room to move. Lovell comes up next to me.

"How come she using someone else's stone?'

"I didn't have one."

"When did you bury her here?"

"After I shot Daddy."

We stand listening to the curses of the guards as limbs break and thorns rip into skin.

"You sure she's here?" one says.

I nod. I know Daddy's in the creek and Momma's here. Somewhere. They're all here. The others – the others that have been killed in the creek – they may have been buried somewhere else, but they're here. All of them. With Momma. They gonna hear what I tell her, too.

A yell from one corner comes. Lovell starts to move but I stay and raise my hands as far as they go toward him, hoping. He shakes his head.

"Just this once," I say. "I don't want her to see me like this."

"Can't do it, Wayne."

We walk over to the stone together.

"All right, Wayne. Here she is. What you wanted," Lovell says as we stop before it. The guards back away and stand with Lovell.

I squat and rub some dirt away from the etched letters. I take some dirt – the dirt I dug in that rain – and hold it in my hands. I open my palms and let it drop back to the ground. I put my dirty hands into my face. The blackness comes. I run inside that blackness, run to that hole, holding her. I run to that creek, to that cleansing water. I run from that store, run. I run. And I run until I fall into that chair.

It is there I say my last words.

Momma, I know you see these chains and this suit. I know you aren't proud. I'm not proud of me, neither. I'm sorry.

I did some good, though. I told them where some girls were buried and they said I could come here and talk to you.

Before, when I came, I was running for my life. Now, Momma, tomorrow, that ends. I'm gonna be put to death – add another one to the line, like Daddy said.

All the stories you told me, Momma, they were true. I saw all of 'em – all the people we killed – when I shot that man and his wife. They came when I shot Daddy too. I promised you I wouldn't but I did. I'm sorry.

I killed Daddy. Left him in that creek and it rose in me. It swallowed me.

Like it swallowed us all, Momma. I'm sorry. This creek has cursed us all, Momma. But my son – I got a son, Momma – he's safe. He's clean, I promise.

I'm going to be clean, too, Momma, I promise. You waited all this time, I know. And it's going to be just like you wanted. It isn't going to kill anymore. It's saving, Momma. The creek's going to save me.

Chapter Eleven

I HEAR THE RATTLING of the door and look up. I usually sleep facing the door – an old superstition. I hear Lovell's voice over the sound of his keys.

"You awake?"

"Yeah."

"I'm gonna open the solid door."

"OK."

"There. Now you can see me."

"Thanks."

I push myself up to sit against the bed.

"How long did I sleep?"

"About two hours I suppose."

"Thanks. What time is it?"

"About one. Wayne, they're gonna come get you soon. They're gonna take you to the barber and to eat what you wanted. But today's your shower day and then you need to put this on before they do."

He hands me a red jumpsuit with a black line down each pant leg. On the back it has the same three letters as my other one – JSP.

"Thanks."

After I dress, he comes in and shackles me and leads me to the shower area. I take off my orange jumpsuit and step under the water flow. I pull my head out and watch water run down my stomach and legs, following the drops all the way to my toes. Just to see the water clean me. I close my eyes when I put my head back under the water. In that instant the darkness comes. I open my eyes but the water shuts them and the darkness comes.

Lovell pokes his head in and tells me to dry off. I put on the new clothes he gave me. The red suit – dark red – fits better. Lovell had given me a new pair of flip-flops.

He sets me back in the cell and left the solid door open.

"They got the steak – all well done. And the macaroni and cheese. They ain't gonna give you any alcohol so I told them to bring some tea from the kitchen. The warden said the dessert was over your $20 limit. But I kept some cake from lunch for you."

"Thanks, Lovell."

He stands close to the door and from my bed I see he has on his court uniform – tie, jacket with a bright badge on the side, and shined shoes.

"You look nice – real professional."

He nods.

I toss my feet to the floor and rub my face with my hands.

"It was real nice of you to let me stay outside longer on Thursday. I'll remember that."

He nods.

"And yesterday – thanks for that."

He nods again and looks down the hall for a second.

"You got the bucket?"

He let me ride with it on the way back.

"Yeah, it's down the hall."

"You got enough?"

"It doesn't take that much, Wayne."

I stand up and take a step toward the door. He backs away a little.

"Maybe you ought to sit back down. When the warden comes, he doesn't like to see you up near the door."

I do. Because I know he's nervous.

"Where they going to bury me?" I ask.

"Well since you ain't got no family, I think they bury you in the pauper's graves behind the prison."

"They going to give me a stone?"

"Not a stone, but a little metal marker."

"You going to dig my hole?"

"No. But I'll see that it's done right – that they treat you good."

He looks down the hall again.

"Hell, Lovell I should be the one looking."

Six hours now but he's the one nervous. They get this way anytime they do it – wanting it to go right and all. And me being the last one in the chair, they don't want to end on a bad one.

"What they going to do with it – the chair – when they done?" I ask.

Nothing from Lovell, who looks down the hall.

"You think Carey will go next?"

He doesn't answer again, looking down that hall.

"Lovell?"

"Maybe."

Then finally the warden comes. He explains to me again about the barber. We can go to the barber once a month if we want. Most everybody goes just to leave the cell. I didn't have much hair from the last visit but this time he was taking it all.

Lovell opens the bars and shackles me. As we walk I notice all the other solid doors are closed. I notice the paint chipping on one of the corners we turn.

They had set the barber up in a hallway with a folding chair and his razor plugged into an outlet. He stood there holding the cloth they put around your neck. Lovell sat me down in the chair and I close my eyes when the razor hit my skull. I could hear her voice. Wayne, you gonna look good for the preacher, like Momma wants.

I always talk to the barber – just about stuff and all. But this time I don't say anything, with the warden there. And he knows why I was getting a shave. He finishes and dusts my head off with a brush. The Velcro rips from behind me and he draws the cloth away. Then he squats down and raises my pant leg just above my shackles. I look down and see shaving cream on my leg.

"What's he doing that for?" I ask.

"Wayne, we talked about this," Lovell says. "It's for the electrode."

The man shaves a small part of my leg with one of those plastic razors and then wipes off the extra cream.

Lovell stands me up and we continue down the same hall, making another turn. He leads me into the visiting room. The warden explained before this was where I could eat and afterwards the reporter would come to talk with me.

I sit down at the table and Lovell unchains my hands. They have an inmate wearing rubber gloves and a hairnet bring me some tea in a paper cup and a Styrofoam tray with two sections – one for the steak and one for the macaroni. I smile when I see I get to use a plastic knife and fork. I press them into the steak on the first cut and break them. Then I get a real knife and fork. Real formal.

The warden steps out of the room and Lovell walks over and stood next to me.

"Need anything?"

I answer without looking up. "Some sauce would be good."

I drink some tea as he looks at the waiter and mouths the order. I get Heinz 57 – which Daddy never liked. When the waiter comes out again, he brings me some cake, too. I pour the sauce over each piece of steak on my fork and eat the noodles one at a time. Then the warden comes back and says I have ten minutes.

I don't know why I ordered steak but it seemed like a nice meal. Carey said he was gonna order two when he goes. I got the macaroni because Momma always made that. This was nothing like hers – she had bread crumbs and two types of cheese. And I wanted a beer – not just any beer – a Budweiser. It's what I drank after I killed Daddy. But the tea was good – always good tea here. I ate the cake, but didn't really want to. It wasn't any good for lunch, either.

When I told Lovell I was finished, the waiter came and cleared the table. They let me sit for a few minutes. Lovell stands beside me, looking out toward the door, through the windows on either side that showed the hallway. I see his fingers. The ends were hard, like they had dead skin on them. He has a scratch on his left hand, right on a knuckle. His fingers are the last things I am going to see.

"Hey Lovell."

He doesn't hear me, looking into the hallway.

"Is there going to be a lot of people?"

"Yeah – always is."

"They going to all watch me?"

"Yeah."

"You going to be with me?"

He looks down at me.

"Yeah, Wayne. I'll be there."

The warden comes in with the reporter. He, too, was dressed nice – suit and tie and shiny shoes. The rag for his glasses looked new, too, poking out of his pocket.

He sits down and pulls a piece of paper out of his jacket. It was a copy of the morning paper. It wasn't the whole paper just what seemed like the front page. There was my picture and the story about me. Killer Set To Die Ready to Go.

He folds up the paper and puts it back in his pocket after I looked it over.

"Did you write that – that about ready to go?"

"No. Some editor. You think it fits?"

I nod. It is strange to see it, though. All across the state after I die this morning everybody will know – know I changed.

"I talked to that family – the parents of those girls you knew – and they said they never knew anything until you said what you said. They asked me to say that whatever you did, they knew you were sorry for it. They said you made it right with them."

I was really making it right with myself.

"The warden told me you had steak. Any good?"

"Yeah. With some sauce."

"You still going to write that book?" I ask.

"This is my final chapter."

"You going to write about my son?"

"If he wants – you want me to?"

I shrug.

"He might like to know how you changed."

I suppose he was right. I wish I could have taken him to the creek to be clean. Momma would have liked that.

"You going to talk about my momma and how she died?"

He nods.

"You going to talk about my daddy?"

"Maybe I'll try to find him. Is he still alive?"

"You won't find him."

"He's got to be somewhere – there's a record of some place he's lived. Then again, he may have died – do you know what happened to him?"

His face floats in the water, floating with all the others, all the others who died there. Sometimes I think Hell isn't where it's really at. Sometimes I think it is the cold bottom of a creek where a killer is drowned by the crying.

I wish he could hear me now.

"He's dead."

"How did you find out?" There was surprise in his voice. "When did he die?"

"He died when I shot him."

"When?"

"Right after he killed Momma. I led him to the creek, had him walk in a few steps, and shot him. What was left in the gun."

"And you left him there?"

"I buried him under a lot of rocks at the bottom of the creek."

"And you never told anyone?"

"Except the preacher the other day. "

"Why did you tell me now?"

"I'm ready to die. I've made it right with everybody. Made it right with myself."

He sighs and flops his tie in his hands.

"Is that when it started – the robberies, all of it?"

I nod and then sink my head a little. I wanted to feel different, feel changed. I wanted to say it like I was sorry.

"You going to tell my son what I did?"

"You want me to?"

"Just tell him his father changed. That his father was clean when he died. You tell him I was clean. Tell him the creek isn't in him. Tell him that."

I wanted it to be true. Like Momma. She wanted my promise to be true, she wanted me not to be like Daddy, like all the others – but she knew I was. She knew I was going to kill him. The reporter wrote it down and then looked back up at me.

"Do you think your son will be proud of you – for changing?"

"I always wanted my momma to be proud of me."

"Do you think she was?"

"I know she is."

I want to tell him about going to see Momma. But if I do I know Lovell might get into trouble.

"I have been wondering since we been talking now – why did you answer my letter? The others... other people on death row always want the media to talk to them. So they can relive it. The real sick ones like that. For them it's like doing it all again. But with you... what made you agree?"

I knew what he meant – those girls were killed again and again in my ears. But I really didn't know why I started telling him or telling Rick. I never wanted to relive any of it. It just always came.

"It was just the changing, I guess."

I look at the clock on the wall beyond the reporter. About six. It was coming soon. The thin black needle was inching toward it.

"You going to be in the room?"

He nods.

"You going to watch?"

"I will."

"When they flip the switch, you going to write down how I look?"

"Yeah."

"Do you think I'll be able to see anything through the bag?"

"Depends – on how dark it is."

When Lovell pulls the bag over my head, I know what I'll see. It's why I've tried to remember so many things. From yesterday. I counted my steps to the barber. And how many noodles I ate. Just to fill my head so I wouldn't see the memories. Dirty clothes. A Korean man. That face in the rearview mirror. A broken tombstone. A piece of paper telling me I am dead.

"I hope it's black, real black in that bag. I don't want to see anything."

"You decided on what you're going to say?"

I shake my head.

"You scared?"

I look down at my fingernails, avoiding the question and the clock.

"Some."

"You think you deserve this?"

"I'm making it right with them."

He turns to look at the clock on the wall. I look at my fingers again.

"I think my time is going to be done here soon. After all you said about your family, I was wondering the people who named that stream Murder Creek – do you think they ever thought you would be sitting here?"

I always thought that marker Momma made me read was about somebody else, somebody dead. But after reading what happened there and then hearing what Momma said all my life, I know now the words were never about somebody else. It's a record of who we are, who I am, who I was.

I could never say it right, but I never forgot what the Indians called the creek: *hesaketv em uewv*. They had it right to begin with. Rick said that to me yesterday when I came back from seeing Momma. Lovell had told him what my plan was for the bucket of water. And he stood in front of my cell and said I had found the waters of life in that creek. Just like the Indians.

So that was my answer to the reporter.

"The guy who called it Murder Creek – one of my kin – I think that he was just trying to make what the Indians did seem worse than what he did. I think Murder Creek was never about any Indian."

He wrote that down and closed his notebook. My last words.

The warden comes in then and tells me my time's up. He says the preacher will be here soon.

Lovell takes me back to my cell. He looks up after locking the door.

"Hey Lovell. Is it scary when they put the bag over you?"

"Some. But I'll be doing that, Wayne. I'll be there."

"Thanks Lovell."

Lovell closes the solid door. I'm against the wall so I bang for Carey. He wakes up.

"What were you dreaming about?" I ask.

"I was drowning in a bowl filled with milk."

Always the same dream.

"The preacher coming by?"

"Lovell said soon."

"The steak good?"

"Yeah – got to get yourself one."

"Two, Wayne. Gonna get me two. With Spaghetti Os."

"Right."

"How's the head feel?"

I run my fingers over my skull.

"Like Lovell's. But the spot on my leg is itching."

We sit in silence for a few moments. Then his toilet flushes.

"I didn't wanna tell you, with you going and all but when you heard me singing with the preacher, that's when I found out."

I knew without asking.

"July 23."

"You got a good chance of getting..."

"We all got no chance, now, with them switching. They gonna be ordering steaks up and down this row for a while."

"Two for you. Two for you."

He didn't laugh.

"It's all right Carey, me going and you going – we all going at some point."

"Man, that paper – he brought me that and I pissed on it, right there. Funny shit, Wayne. But just now, standing there with my... Just holding my... I'm thinking how many more am I gonna get? How many more days? 45. That's how many."

I hear him kick the metal under his mattress. His next words come muffled – like he was speaking with his hands over his face.

"How does it feel?"

"How does what feel?"

"Telling all that – telling them – that reporter, the preacher – telling them all the shit you did? Telling about them girls?"

I look up to the ceiling. I knew Carey was staring at the same concrete heaven.

"Hey Carey, can I tell you something?"

"Sure, man, any shit you want."

"I'm scared."

He didn't say anything.

"I thought it would go away when I started talking. But it's still there – all of it. And when that bag comes, when Lovell puts that bag on me, it's going to come again. So it don't feel no different."

"Can I tell you something? When I close my eyes, that cop comes. It isn't like what you see – he's alive, running after me. Like I hadn't shot him. He doesn't have hands. Just bones. And his legs are something else. Like the skin is coming off. Weird Halloween shit. And his face – sometimes when I see it, it's mine. My face coming after me. Then I shoot – shoot me. Like I was looking in a mirror. Me killing me."

I've seen that mirror, too.

"Hey Carey, will you do something for me?"

"Yeah."

"Tell me what you look like."

"What?"

"Tell me what you look like."

"Why? You know, man, already. I'm uglier than..."

"But tell me again. So I'll have something to see when the bag covers me. Something instead of..."

I hear the jangling of the keys. The solid door opens and the warden and Lovell and some other guards are there. There is no time left. The six is coming.

"It's time to go, Wayne. We gonna take you to the holding cell where you can talk to the preacher."

I stand up and look at the red suit. I step toward the door and feel the wet spots on my flip-flops. I step in front of Lovell. I put my hands together but he shakes his head. As I walk through the solid door, I stop. "Hey Carey, do you believe in heaven?"

"Yeah, man, all that shit. Yeah."

"I'll put in a good word."

"I'm going to hell, Wayne. But I'll tell your daddy you said hello."

I pass the warden. Another guard leads me down the row. All the solid doors are closed but voices without faces say their goodbyes.

We walk down a long hallway, past the visiting room, and then turn right. We get to a door on the left that stands next to a wall. Lovell unlocks the door and I see Rick sitting in his folding chair. There is one of those small metal beds chained to the wall for me. Past Rick is another door – the door. My last door.

"The preacher here gonna sit with you while everything is getting ready," Lovell says.

I sit down. The room is small – smaller than my cell.

"It's a little after 5, if you're wondering," Rick says.

"I was. Thanks." I look at the door. The six is coming.

The door has a big, round handle, like on a boat. The room's green all around and there's a toilet and sink like in my old cell.

"On the other side of that door, Wayne, is the last room."

It is the last of the lasts. My last steps. My last seat. My last breath. I pull my shoulders down and hang my hands between legs, putting my arms on my thighs. Rick pulls his chair in front of me. He puts a hand on my head and another on my knee.

"Look at me."

I shake my head.

"God has something to say to you."

I look up.

"He isn't going to let you die alone. He isn't going to let you die scared."

I nod.

"He is here."

His hand reaches up to cover my eyes. My hand meets his.

"I'm scared to see..."

"He is here."

I kneel in front of the white door.

You are with me, now.

I will sprinkle clean water on you and you shall be clean.

This water that causeth the curse I have healed. There shall not be from there any more death.

It is finished.

The hand has left and the voice trails away too. I remain in the blackness, the darkness where God has found me. In my last hour. In my last prayer.

The door creaks open. I take a step toward it. For a second I pause. But there is no stopping at the door. There is no more time for waiting.

The room is a square of blocks, green, one after another. A large wooden chair with belts on the arms and legs and what looks like a frying pan hanging over where my head is going to go. Deep varnish.

Lovell's hands put me in.

In front of me a large window. The microphone hanging from the ceiling. Lovell squats to tighten the straps on my legs.

My wrists shiver from the cold wood – or is it shaking? Lovell grabs my right arm and motions for another person to hold it down while he tightens the strap. Then the other just the same. Giant belts – or are my eyes getting smaller?

My ears – they're working. A whisper.

You doing good Wayne, real good.

The belly strap takes away my breath. The leg belt locks me in. I can't move. My thighs can't tighten. I can't turn my wrists. I have moved for the very last time.

It's gonna be all right, Wayne. All right.

My left pant peg is yanked up. Lovell, bent over, is rubbing some jelly on it. A cotton circle with a wire sticks. I follow it as far as my eyes allow behind me. I turn my head and see the window before me. I see people have gathered on the bank. In white dresses and rolled up sleeves. Here to watch me die. Here to watch me get clean.

I am sorry. For everything. I am ready.

The fingers slip the blackness over me. I see my son – or is it me? – running in the creek, the faces in the reflection broken, erased from the surface.

The preacher places his hands on my head. I do not struggle as he tightens his grip. I want to be clean.

Water falls down my head, over my eyes, past the cheek with the tears, and into my mouth.

The preacher whispers, whispers, whispers. I baptize you in the name of the father, the son, and the holy...

And I give up my ghost, opening my eyes to the waters of life.

About the Author

Dr. Matthew Boedy is a professor in the English department at the University of North Georgia. He lives in Gainesville, Georgia. This is his first novel.